D0784940

She removes a beckoning finger of hair that has become stuck to her cheek and comes towards me. Oh my gawd! I always reckoned it was like this in the Turkish baths. Either that or Bernard Dillons locking you in the steam cabinets . . . 'Hang on a minute,' I say. 'I think there's something you ought to know.'
'We know all about you,' she says cheerfully.
Her words strike cold terror into my heart . . .
'I don't want to give offence,' I say, 'but I'm not in the mood. The heat, the lack of food. I've hardly got the strength to pull my socks up . . . I think I'll nip back to my room for a lie down.' . . .
'This way.' She pulls open a door and I start scrambling up some steps before I know what I am doing. Suddenly, before me, is a small, deep pool. I can tell by looking at it that it is very, very cold . . .
'I'm going to help you,' says Miss T. calmly. 'I'm going to soothe you, calm you, ease your fears and bring you pleasure all in one delicious experience.'

## Also by Timothy Lea

CONFESSIONS FROM THE POP SCENE

Timothy Lea

# Confessions from a Health Farm

Futura Publications Limited

A Futura Book

First published in Great Britain in 1974
by Futura Publications Limited



ISBN 0 8600 7099 9
Printed in Great Britain by
Hazell Watson & Viney Ltd
Aylesbury, Bucks

Futura Publications Limited
49 Poland Street,
London W1A 2LG

# CONTENTS

# CHAPTER 1

**In which Sidney explains the rudiments of the beauty business and Timmy experiences some of them at the hands – and other things – of shapely Wanda Zonker.**

'I got a post card from Nutter, today,' says Sid, pushing away his tea cup as if he never wanted to see one again – with Mum's tea you feel like that.

'That's nice. How is he?' I say.

'Difficult to tell. Most of it has been crossed out by the censors. He seems a bit under the weather, though – not surprising when you think how much it rains over there.' Sid laughs heartlessly.

I pick up the postcard: 'The paddy fields, Ho-lung-ti.'

'It looks nice, doesn't it,' I say. 'The mountains and all that in the background.'

'Blooming marvellous,' says Sid. 'I envy those boys, really I do. Doing away with National Service was the worst thing we ever did in this country. I remember how disappointed I was when they stopped it just before I was due to be called up.'

'Why didn't you sign on, then?'

Sid looks uncomfortable. 'It wouldn't have been the same, would it? I mean, I wanted to go in with all my mates, didn't I?'

'They could have signed on as well, Sid.'

Sid shakes his head. 'Not everybody feels the same as I do about this septic isle, Timmo. I've only got to hear the opening bars of "Land Of Hope And Glory" and I'm rummaging through Rosie's Kleenex.'

I tear my mind away from this affecting thought and examine the postcard. The first word is scratched out and followed by 'you' and an exclamation mark. Then comes another 'you' followed by three words that have been crossed out followed by a double exclamation mark. Fortunately, though it would have been unfortunately, had I been of a sensitive disposition, I can still read one of the crossed out words.

'I don't reckon it was the blokes in Taiwan that censored this, Sid,' I say. 'It must have been our lot. Nutter isn't half having a go at you.'

Not that I blame the poor sod. If you read *Confessions from the Pop Scene* (published by Futura Publications) you will recall that Nutter and a group called 'Kipper' were rail-roaded out to Taiwan, that used to be Formosa like Alvin Stardust used to be Shane Fenton, by Sidney Noggett who still is my brother-in-law. They thought they were going to promote their chart-busting record but Sidney had arranged for them to promote the Taiwanese war effort by signing them on for five years in Chiang-Kai-Shek's army. Sidney does not usually go to this amount of trouble for people unless they are costing him money and there is little doubt that 'Kipper' were becoming an expensive luxury.

Sid picks up the postcard. 'It's a nice stamp, though, isn't it? I'll save that for little Jason.'

'You never think about them, do you?' I accuse. 'Thousands of miles from home and with none of their own kind near them.'

'They never have any of their own kind near them,' says Sid bitterly. 'You tell me one person who is as greedy, lazy and useless as they are.'

'I don't want to hurt your feelings, Sid,' I say after I have thought about it for a minute.

Sidney waggles his finger at me. 'That's very naughty, Timmo. You know how sensitive I am.'

I take a long look at the poor little suffering tea leaves at the bottom of my cup and decide to change the subject. 'What's this new idea of yours, Sid?' I ask.

'It's a gold mine,' says Sid.

My heart sinks. I can just see it. Some clapped out National Coal Board reject that Sid has been conned in to buying. Broken down lifts, flooded galleries, no pit head baths, worked out seams. And who will end up thousands of feet below the earth with a mickey mouse torch tied to his bonce and a kiddy's spade in his mit? That's right, yours bleeding truly.

'I'm sorry, Sid,' I say. 'I don't want any part of it.'

'But you haven't heard what it is yet!'

'I don't care about the details. I'm not going down any mine.'

Sidney claws the air in exasperation. 'I was talking metaphysically, wasn't I? I don't mean a real gold mine. I never fancied mines after I saw *Shaft*.

'*Shaft* wasn't about mining, Sid.'

'You mean that big, black bloke didn't have coal dust all over his mug?'

'No, Sid! He was born like that.' Honestly, you worry sometimes, don't you? They say that there are over a million illiterates in the country and I reckon that they lie pretty thick around Scraggs Lane.

'Oh,' says Sid. 'That explains a lot of things.'

'What about the new idea?' I say.

Saying that to Sid is like striking a match to find a gas leak, but somehow I can't help myself. I have been stuck with Sid for so long that I cannot break away. Like a junkie begging for his fix I must know what half-baked scheme the Maestro of Muddle has come up with now.

Sidney leans back nonchalantly and rests his elbow in the frying pan that Mum has left on top of the cooker. Like everything on the cooker, including the rings, it is coated in half an inch of grease and is well equipped to become the first item of hardware to swim the Channel. Sid's safari jacket therefore has to make a quick trip into the interior of the washing machine before the great white hunter can continue.

'Do you know what is the biggest problem facing this country today?' says Sid.

'Inflation?' I say. I mean, I listen to the party political broadcasts, don't I? There is no bleeding alternative.

'In a manner of speaking,' says Sid, slightly downcast. 'Obesity was the word I had in mind.

Well, it is a free country, isn't it? I can't tell him what words to put in his mind, although they would have to be blooming small to fit into that tiny little space. I would have thought that you needed to fold 'obesity' in half to get it in without touching the sides.

'Oh yes,' I say.

'You don't know what obesity means, do you?' says Sid triumphantly.

'No,' I say. 'That's why you used it, isn't it?'

'It means being fat.' Sidney looks me up and down critically.

'About ninety percent of the people in this country weigh too much.'

'That's amazing,' I say, stretching out my hand for another doughnut.

'You for instance,' says Sid. 'It's disgusting to see a bloke of your age falling apart at the seams.'

'What are you rabbiting on about,' I say. 'I'm in perfect physical condition. I could run rings round you any day of the week.'

'You must have put on a stone since you came out of the army,' continues Sid. 'You've got the beginnings of a paunch and there are rolls of fat building up round your waist. I can't imagine how you do it. Living here I'd have thought that you had a bloody marvellous incentive not to eat.'

Sid is, of course, referring to Mum's cooking. He has never had any time for her since she tried to boil a tin of sardines. Mind you, she is diabolical in the kitchen and maybe that is why I eat so much. I am forced to have a go at the nosh she dishes up and I also eat between meals to take away the taste and give myself a little reward.

'You're no oil painting,' I say.

'I'm fitter than you are, mate. Feel that.'

'Sidney, please!'

'I meant my stomach, didn't I? Don't take the piss.'

'I don't want to feel your stomach, Sid.'

'Go on!' Sid is speaking through clenched teeth as he tenses his muscles. Reluctantly, I stretch out a hand.

'It feels like a pregnant moggy,' I say.

Sid does not respond well to this suggestion. 'Bollocks!' he says. 'Like ribs of steel, my stomach muscles. You try hitting them.'

'Sidney, please! This is bloody stupid.'

'Hard as you like. Go on!' Sidney stands up and swells out his belly invitingly.

'I don't want to hurt you, Sid,' I say.

'You can't hurt me! That's what I'm trying to tell you, you berk! I'm in shape, I'm fit, I'm – uuuuuurgh!'

I give him a little tap in the stomach and he collapses on the floor spluttering and groaning. Mum comes in.

'He hasn't been at the bread and butter pudding, has he?' she says, alarmed.

'No, Mum.'

'Thank goodness for that. You were right, you know. Some of those sultanas were blue bottles. I think I'll have to throw it away. It's such a fiddling job picking them all out.' She looks down at Sid. 'What's the matter with him?'

'He was showing me how fit he is,' I say.

'He hit me when I wasn't ready,' wheezes Sid. 'That's what happened to Houdini.'

'Oh dear,' says Mum. 'That doesn't sound very nice. I wouldn't stay down there if I was you. It's not very clean.'

Sid drags himself to his feet and slumps into a chair. Mum was right. He looks like the inside of a carpet sweeper.

'You did that on purpose,' he grunts.

'Of course I did,' I say. 'You told me to.'

'You haven't put anything in the washing machine, have you?' says Mum.

I sense Sid stiffen. 'What's wrong with it?' he says.

'I don't know,' says Mum. 'The man hasn't been yet. I think it spins round too fast. Either that or there is a rough edge in there.'

Sid springs to the machine and presses the programme switch. He wrenches open the door and a couple of gallons of water thwack against the far wall.

'I didn't notice that was in there,' I say. I am referring to the well-worn chammy leather with pockets.

Sid groans. 'Eighteen quid that cost.'

'Blimey! That's your safari jacket, isn't it?' I say.

'Don't sound so bleeding cheerful,' snarls Sid. 'You ought to have put an "out of order" sign on it.'

'I did,' says Mum. 'But I moved it to the bread and butter pudding.'

'Gordon Bennet!' Sid covers his face with his hands.

'Sid has got a new idea,' I say, deciding that it is time for another change of subject. 'It's something to do with fat people.'

'I'm going to classes now,' says Mum. 'Do you think I look any different?'

'You look a bit paler, Mum,' I say.

'Don't say that! I was thinking how well I looked. I've lost half a stone, you know.'

'Where did you lose it, Mum?' I ask.

'Round the bum, mostly,' says Mum with an honesty I could have done without.

'I didn't mean that,' I say hurriedly before she can impart any more revelations. It's not nice listening to your parents talk about their bodies, is it? It is bad enough having to look at them.

'The Lady Beautiful Health Clinic,' says Sid. 'That's what I'm on about. More and more people are becoming worried about the condition of their bodies. You mother is only following a trend.'

'You want to be careful, Mum,' I say. 'You remember what happened when you tried that yoga.' I have to suppress a shudder when I think about it. Everywhere you went in the house there would be Mum standing on her head against one of the walls. And often without any clothes on! Yoga Bare, that's what Sid used to call her. Luckily she bombed out in the Padandgushtasana position and we did not hear any more about it.

Further discussion is interrupted by the sound of the front door bell.

'Who's that?' says Sid whose reaction to the unexpected reveals a permanently guilty conscience.

'Probably Dad's lost his front door key,' says Mum. She leaves the kitchen and pads off to have a peep through the front room curtains. A couple of minutes later she returns.

'There's a gorilla standing on the front door step,' she says.

'A stuffed one? With Dad?' says Sid.

'No it's carrying a brief case,' says Mum.

'Probably something to do with one of those soap powder promotions. Have you got a packet of Tide in the house?'

'No!' says Mum, getting all agitated. 'You keep him talking while I nip out and get one.'

I grab hold of her just before she disappears out of the back door.

'Hold on, Mum. We don't know it's Tide. It could be any of them. You don't want to spend a fortune for nothing.'

There is another long blast on the front door bell followed by frenzied banging.

'Sounds like your father,' says Mum.

'Let's have a look.' I follow Sid into the front room and peel back the yellowing net curtains. There, indeed, is a gorilla carrying a briefcase. It looks towards the window and jabs its finger at its stomach.

'I think it's trying to say it's hungry,' I say.

'No, you berk. It's trying to say its zipper has jammed. Don't you recognise your own father? He looks more like himself in that than he does in a suit. No gorilla ever stands like that.' A small crowd of onlookers has assembled at the gate and the gorilla makes a familiar gesture to them.

'Yes, that's Dad all right,' I say. 'I suppose we'd better let him in.'

'About bleeding time!' says Dad's muffled voice as he charges through the door. 'A man could suffocate in one of these things.'

'Now he tells us,' says Sid. 'Another couple of minutes on the doorstep and all our troubles would have been over.'

'Belt up, sponger!' croaks Dad. 'Help us get it off for gawd's sake!'

We struggle with the zip and eventually manage to release an escape hatch for Dad.

'Phew!' says Sid. 'Are you sure the gorilla isn't still in there with you? It doesn't half pong around here.'

'That's the bloody tube for you,' says Dad. 'You want to try strap hanging from Charing Cross in that thing and see how you feel.'

'Did you swing from strap to strap, Dad?' asks Sid, lowering his voice and beating his chest. 'Me, father Lea. King of de Northern Line.'

'Shut your face!' snaps Dad. 'It's a lovely thing. I couldn't let it go in the incinerator.'

I feel I should point out that my revered parent works in the lost property office and is inclined to 'save' certain articles which he considers might be lost to Sir Kenneth Clark, or handed in to the keeping of undesirables – e.g. their rightful owners.

'I don't understand why you wore it,' says Mum.

'It seemed the best way of getting it home,' says Dad, mopping his brow. 'I'd have looked bloody silly carrying it, wouldn't I? This way I was anonymous so nobody knew who I was. The coon who was collecting the tickets at Clapham South took one look at me and started running across the common.'

'I bet you weren't even wearing the head-piece, then,' I say cheerfully.

'At least he could run,' says Sid. 'Look at you. Puffing and blowing like an old grampus. You underline what I've been saying to Timmy and Mum. You're all overweight and unfit. The whole country is dragging round tons of surplus weight. That's why we're in the mess we are at the moment. Pare off those extra pounds and the natural vitality will start flooding through your veins.'

'Sounds disgusting,' says Dad. 'Is my tea ready yet?'

'You're the worst of the lot,' says Sid sternly. 'There's a permanent depression in the middle of the armchair made by your great fat arse while you watch telly. The only exercise you ever take is jumping to conclusions.'

'How dare you!' bellows Dad. 'This is my house you're standing in. You keep your filthy tongue under control. I don't have to listen to this.'

'Look at him!' says Sid. 'That's a sick face, that is, mark my words. See those treacherous little blue veins running through that sea of scarlet porridge? That's not healthy. That's a face living on borrowed time.'

'He doesn't look very good, does he?' says Mum, peering into Dad's mug. 'Still you've got to remember he's been like that for years.'

'Stop talking about me as if I'm not here!' squawks Dad.

'That's it exactly,' says Sid. 'Very prophetic words. Soon you *won't* be here. You've got to get a grip on yourself. Like I said, you're living on borrowed time.'

'If you ever lend me any, you won't see it back again in a hurry,' says Dad bitterly.

'What are you getting at, Sid?' I say. 'Are you starting some kind of keep-fit class?'

Sidney's lip curls contemptuously. 'Much more than that,' he says. 'Keeping fit is just the tip of the iceberg. It's the whole spectrum of physical and mental welfare that I want to embrace.'

'Watch your language in front of my wife,' says Dad.

Something tells me that Sid has been got at. He does not normally come out with sentences like that unless his chips were wrapped in the Weekend Section of the Sunday Times.

'Who told you about that?' I ask.

'Wanda Zonker,' says Sid as if he is glad to get it off his chest. 'She's a remarkable woman. She's a beautician and health food specialist. I'm thinking of getting together with her to open a health farm.'

'Where's the money coming from?' says Dad.

'I've got a bit tucked away,' says Sid.

'So you've just told us,' says Dad. 'I was asking about the money.'

Sid does not take kindly to the implication behind this remark.

'Shut your mouth, you disgusting old rat bag!' he snaps. 'Rosie will probably be coming in with us. There's nothing underhand about what I'm doing. Nothing compared to nicking stuff from the lost property office and keeping the hallstand full of filthy Swedish magazines.'

'How did you know they were Swedish, clever shanks!?' exults Dad. 'You've been peeping, haven't you?'

'Please!' I say, desperate to raise the standard of argument a few notches above crutch level. 'Can't we forget about "Swedish Spanking Party, Volumes 1–5" and concentrate on something more intellectually stimulating?'

'You were at them and all, were you?' says Dad. 'Marvellous, isn't it? I only bring them home for the articles and I'm being branded as some kind of pervert.'

'What articles?' says Sid. '"How spanking saved my marriage"? "Spanking round the world"? "Cooking for spankers"?'

'Nothing like that!' snorts Dad. 'I mean the articles by famous living men of letters. I don't look at the pictures.'

'Yeah. Smoke rises from his fingers, he turns the pages over so fast,' sneers Sid.

'"Wanda Zonker"?' says Mum. 'She foreign, is she?' There is a strong note of disapproval in her voice. Mum has been around long enough to know that foreigners cause most of the trouble in the world.

'Yes, Mum. She's a Lithuanian.'

'Oh.' Mum does not sound as if that is the best news she has heard since the end of World War Two. 'Where's that?'

Sid looks round the room and shrugs his shoulders. 'I don't know, Mum.'

'I've never met anyone who did know,' says Mum suspiciously. 'You want to watch those Lithuanians. There's a lot of them about and nobody knows where they come from. You want to ask her if you see her again.'

'If she says Peckham, he's not going to know whether she's telling the truth or not,' says Dad.

'It's definitely abroad,' says Mum.

'"Next week, our panel of experts will be discussing Euthanasia – does it come too late?"' says Sid in his posh announcer voice.

'Come on, Timmo. I'll go bonkers if I hang around here much longer. I'm nipping round to see Wanda now. I'll introduce you.'

'You watch yourself,' says Dad. 'Don't sign anything.'

'Tell you what I'll do,' says Sid. 'When it's all fixed up I'll give you a fortnight's free treatment. That'll open your eyes – your pores, your bowels, everything!'

'Don't be disgusting!' Dad's voice echoes after us as we bundle out of the front door.

Sid rubs his hands together and a far away look comes into his eyes. 'Ooh. I wouldn't half like to get him in one of those dry heat cabinets,' he says. 'I'd turn the bleeding knob up to maximum and watch his nut turn scarlet. Twenty minutes later there would be nothing left but a puddle in the bottom of the cabinet.'

'Sid! Please! That's my old man you're talking about.'

Sid shakes his head. 'I'm sorry. I keep forgetting that he's a human being.' Sid has been bashing the horror movies a bit lately and I think that they have an unfortunate effect on him. He is always knocking back his cha with a maniacal laugh and saying, 'Today, Clapham. Tomorrow the world!' I could belt him sometimes.

'Where does this tart live?' I ask.

An expression of pain flashes across Sid's features. 'Watch it,' he says. 'She's quality, this bird. Refined. You know what I mean?'

'She washes her hands before she goes to the karsi?'

Sid shakes his head. 'Don't take the piss, Timmo. She's living in reduced circumstances at the moment but she's still a lady.'

'How did you meet her?' I ask.

'Down the whelk stall in Northcote Road.'

'Oh yes. Very salubrious,' I say. 'Washing them down with a glass of bubbly, was she?'

'Whelks happen to be one of the great health foods,' says Sidney loftily. 'You wouldn't cocoa some of the things whelks can do for you.'

'I know what they do for me,' I say. 'And when you see them they look as if they've already done it.'

'Gordon Bennett! You're disgusting, you are. You take after your old man, there's no doubt about it.'

'Leaving the whelks to one side,' I say. 'What is this bird doing at the moment?'

'She's practising her craft,' says Sid. 'She's a fully qualified masseuse as well as all the other things. She's got a string of initials after her name long enough to spell out your monnicker.'

All the time we are rabbiting, Sid is pushing the Rover 2000 towards Battersea Park and the river – I don't mean literally, though with the price of petrol what it is today you could be excused for wondering.

'I think it's very nice round here,' I say. 'All those trees and the kids digging up the snow drops.'

'Oh it is,' says Sid. 'But it's not what she's used to. Back in Druskininkai, things were different.'

'I imagine they would be,' I say philosophically.

'Here we are.' Sid stops outside a block of flats facing the park and we get out. The column of bell pushes looks like the buttons on a giant's waistcoat but the front door is open and Sid sweeps over the threshold and heads for the stairs.

It is funny, but I have never visited anybody in a block of flats who did not live either in the basement or right at the bleeding top. Sometimes I think that the floors in between are used for storing old furniture. There is never any sign of life on them. Not so the top floor of Porchester Mansions. The whole place is vibrating and the squeaking skylight sets your teeth on edge, the noise it is making.

'She must have a client,' says Sid.

'If she does embalming she could have another one,' I pant. 'Blimey, those stairs don't half knacker you.'

'Because you're so bleeding unfit,' says Sid contemptuously. 'Look at me I'm hardly out of breath. It's all a question of diet and a few exercises.'

I take a quick shufti at Clapham's answer to Paul Newman and I have to confess that he does not look in bad nick. Maybe Madam Zonker knows a thing or two.

Just as that moment there is a long drawn out moan that quite puts the mockers on me. I am not surprised that the pigeon which has landed on the skylight relieves itself. I feel a bit edgy myself.

'What's that?' I say.

'Dunno,' says Sid. 'She seems to have finished anyway.'

The shuddering and shaking has certainly stopped and no sooner has Sid stepped towards the door than it swings open. Revealed to my hungry mince pies is a handsome looking bird wearing a cross between a housecoat and a judo robe. She has short hair and sharp, determined features.

'Hello, Sidney sweetie,' she says. 'You have not seen the milkman, have you? He gets later every day. Henry wants his Ovaltine.' Her accent is very good but you can tell that she is not British. She leans forward to look down the stairs and I can see that her knockers would make a lovely pair of bookends if you could think of the right item to put between them.

'I haven't,' says Sid. 'Wanda, I'd like to introduce my brother-in-law, Timothy Lea. He's very interested in physical culture though you might not believe it to look at him.'

'Charmed,' I say.

Wanda smiles and I notice that she has a few gold teeth sprinkled around her cake hole. 'Likewise,' she says. 'Come in. My session with Sir Henry is over.' She raises the voice when she says the last bit and I get the impression that she is giving someone a message.

I look over her shoulder and there is an elderly geezer adjusting his tie in front of the mirror.

'Your shirt's hanging out at the back,' I say helpfully.

The bloke turns round and – blimey! I recognise that face. I saw him on 'Midweek'. Not for long though, because I was looking for the wrestling. Maybe it was the wrestling? No, it couldn't have been. Some of them look a bit past it but not as far gone as this geezer. He could rupture himself climbing through the ropes.

'Thank you,' he says looking very uncomfortable.

'I always find that's happened when I've been to the karsi,' I say, trying to put him at his ease.

'Karsi?' says the bloke.

'Bog, shit-house,' I say, helpfully. 'I always feel a bit of a berk when somebody points it out.'

Who is he? I know I've seen him. If he was on the telly after ten o'clock he must be a politician. Oh yes, that's right! He's the minister for something. If I can get his autograph I will know who he is. Mum will be impressed, too. He is wearing a waistcoat so he must be a Conservative. Mum has a secret hankering for them. I am quite partial myself. I mean, they have all the money, don't they?

'I am afraid that there is no Ovaltine, today,' says Wanda, picking up a black mask from the carpet.

'I must have a word with you,' murmurs the man.

'Call me later.' Wanda plucks a piece of fluff from the man's suit.

'I've got to have those negatives!'

He sounds really worked up about it. Looking at him I reckon that he must be one of Miss Zonker's newer clients. There is little physical evidence that she has taken him in hand. He looks far too slack and flabby.

'Can I have your autograph?' I say in what is intended to be my friendly voice.

'On a blank cheque, I suppose?!' snaps Sir Henry.

'That'll do if you haven't got a piece of paper,' I say. 'Hold on a minute. You can use the back of –'

I break off when I see what I have picked up. It is a photograph of a man on a bed with two girls, one of whom definitely hails from dusky climes, as they say. Both ladies seem to be on very good terms with the gentleman in question and a good time is being had by all. It is not the photograph I would have chosen for my Christmas card to the Archbishop of Canterbury but I can see that it might have a fairly broad appeal to some sections of the market.

Sir Henry blushes, as well he might. 'I'd hardly have recognised you from that angle,' I say.

'You should see some of the others,' says Wanda. 'Who knows? Perhaps you will.'

'Wanda –!'

Sir Henry follows our hostess to the door and I hear his voice continuing to plead with her.

'Minister of Defence!' I say.

'Not any more,' says Sidney. 'They swop around so much these days, I lose track.'

'He didn't give me his autograph, did he?' I say. 'Mum will be disappointed.'

'Don't worry. Wanda will get it for you later,' says Sid. 'You can have the whole cabinet if you want them.'

'They're all physical fitness fanatics, are they?' I splutter. 'You wouldn't think it to look at them.'

'Half an hour with Wanda makes new men of them,' says Sid.

'That's why I want to set her up somewhere. She's got the technique and she's got the contacts. She can't cope with the demand here.'

'I think he's beginning to see the light,' says Wanda coming in to the room and opening the top drawer of a filing cabinet. 'Drink, anyone?' She looks me up and down and darts her tongue between her lips. 'We'll have to whittle a few pounds off you, won't we?'

'Why?' I say.

'Because if you are going to be one of our hygienists you must be seen to be practising what you preach. Your body is the best advertisement for Inches Limited.'

'That's the name of the firm,' says Sid. 'Clever, isn't it? We're negotiating with Sir Henry for the use of his country seat, Long Hall.'

'Shortly to be renamed Beauty Manor. It's a residential course, you see?'

'Sort of,' I say. They are going a bit fast for me.

Wanda gives Sid a meaningful glance. 'I think you had better leave us, Sidney sweetie. I want to show Timmy my credentials and give him a few tests.'

'Oh yes?' I clear my throat noisily.

'All right,' says Sid. 'Have you got any films to be developed?'

'Yes,' says Wanda. 'And this time, don't take them to Boots. The address is on the label.'

'Oh yes,' says Sid, blushing. 'I got some very old-fashioned looks when I went to collect them. Fancy dressing up a policeman in a wig. If I hadn't seen his hobnail boots sticking out from underneath the perfume counter –'

'Yes, yes. Very distressing,' says Miss Zonker waving Sid towards the door. 'It will teach you to be more careful next time.'

Sid nods at me. 'See you later, Timmo.'

'Tra la, Sid.'

The door closes on my brother-in-law and Wanda Zonker subjects me to her penetrating gaze. 'I'm sorry,' she says. 'But I have to scrutinise you.'

Hello! I might have guessed there would be a catch in it. Sidney never said anything about that.

'You look alarmed,' says Miss Z.

'It's what you were talking about,' I say. 'I don't fancy it.

I might want to have children one day and I've heard there's no going back.'

Miss Zonker looks puzzled. 'Your meaning escapes me,' she says. 'Perhaps I had better set your mind at rest by revealing some of my parts' – in fact she says 'past' but she gives me a nasty turn for a moment. 'I have studied in all the great salons of Europe: Lausanne, Madrid, Stockholm, Paris, Budleigh Salterton. Physical dancing, rhythmical massage, remedial culture, or any combination of the three. I am a founder member of the Volcanic Mud Institute and the Wax Lyrical and have received diplomas from the Papuan Cosmetologists Institute, the Greek National Electrolysis Society and the C.B.I.'

'That's amazing,' I say. 'It's practically a science, isn't it?'

Miss Zonker's face clouds over. 'What do you mean "practically"? We are scientists fighting the war against physical imperfection.'

'But you don't have any medical qualifications, do you?'

'Medical qualifications?' Miss Z. practically holds the words at arms length with one hand while applying contractual pressure to her hooter with the other. 'Our field of activity is so enormous as to defy restriction. There is no part of the mental or physical process that I will not grapple with.' Her breasts heave when she says it and her eyes blaze. I can see that I have touched on something she feels strongly about. 'Before we go any further there is one question that I must ask you.'

'My cards are stamped up to date,' I say.

'Are you frightened of the human body?'

This was not the question I was expecting but it is still pretty easy. 'No,' I say.

'Good.' Miss Zonker suddenly unties the sash of her robe and – eek! She has shed her threads before you can say Roger Carpenter. 'It's only flesh, isn't it? Shoulders, breasts, hips –'

'Yes!' I gulp. 'But –'

'Nothing to be ashamed of. We're all the same underneath

these dust sheets we call clothes. Take your trousers off.'

Oh dear. I never feel at my happiest when I am up against one of these forward ladies – especially when they come from somewhere in Eastern Europe. You never know what they've been used to, do you?

'Is that really necessary?' I say.

'If you reveal signs of an inhibited nature you will be no good to us at Beauty Manor. Think of yourself as a sculptor and human flesh as your clay.'

I try to think about it but I find it difficult. Maybe it is because Miss Zonker is wrestling with my zipper. My, but she is a strong girl. She grits her teeth and – wheeeeeeeeeeh! The opening at the front of my trousers now goes down to my knee.

'So sorry,' she says. 'Now you will have to take them off.'

'They're not even split down the seam,' I say miserably. 'I've only had them a couple of weeks. They were French.'

Miss Zonker removes a screen and starts fiddling with a large stills camera. 'At Beauty Manor you will wear a toga,' she says. 'Right. Just a couple of snaps for the album. We intend to keep a case history of each of our employees. Perhaps you wouldn't mind posing with that discus.'

'Sidney didn't discus this with me,' I say wittily. Miss Zonker does not say anything. I expect that, being foreign, she finds it difficult to understand our British sense of humour. 'How's this for the pose?' I say.

'Very nice,' she says. 'But I think it would be better if you took the discus out of your mouth. You look like one of those African women with a plate lip.'

'Just trying to make it more interesting,' I say. 'How about this?'

'That's much better. There's only one thing. It loses a lot with you standing there in your shirt and underpants. The socks don't help a lot, either.'

'I don't like them much, myself,' I say. 'My gran gave them to me. You know what it's like?'

'Take everything off,' says Miss Z. firmly. 'I want you

naked.' She starts clicking on spot lights and I have to shield my eyes against the dazzle. 'Come on.' I respond to the tone of brisk efficiency in her voice and start sliding down my Y-fronts. After all, she is a professional, isn't she? If she has cabinet ministers on her books she must be above suspicion. Funny about that photograph, though. I must talk to her about that.

'Shove it up by your ear,' she says.

'I beg your pardon?'

'The discus.'

Oh. For a moment I thought we were on to the remedial contortions.

'This is just for the record, is it?' I say.

'That's right. Bend your knee a bit. That's lovely. Of course, we might get a cover shot out of it.'

'A cover shot?'

' "Butch Male on the Rampage", "Health and Dexterity", something like that.'

'But I'm not like that!' I squeak. It's funny how your voice always breaks at the wrong moment, isn't it?

'It doesn't matter. Nobody's going to know. It's going to make money and that's beautiful.'

'Is it?'

Wanda Zonker speaks what I later learn is one of the great truths of the beauty business.

'*Anything* that makes money is beautiful,' she says, almost reproachfully. 'Drop your shoulder and turn a bit more to the right. You're showing too much puppy fat. We'll have to work at those inches, won't we?' Her voice suddenly goes all husky and her shadow falls across one of the lights. 'You're still tense, aren't you?' She is now standing so close to me that her bristols are brushing my shoulder.

'I'm not used to this caper,' I say.

'It's the sex thing, isn't it?' she says.

'Not exactly,' I say.

'You've no need to be ashamed. It's a fairly common

hang up.' While she talks, her fingers are brushing against my hang down. 'I come up against it every day.'

'Really?' I say. 'Can I put this thing somewhere for a moment? My arm is getting tired.'

'Of course.' Miss Zonker brushes her lips against one of my biceps. 'I think it would be a good idea if we broke off for a bit.' Percy is now in a very breakable condition and I clear my throat nervously. Miss Z. moves her hands to my shoulders and I breathe easier. 'You're thinking of me as a sex object, I can tell.' She looks down between our bodies and we both know what she is talking about. 'I think maybe we'd better get this thing out of the way, don't you?'

I am not quite certain what 'thing' she is talking about but I am too shy to ask. That is why I learned so little at school. If I had my time again I would always ask.

'Uuum,' I say, to show that I have been thinking about it. 'Whatever you think is best.'

'I don't want a sound working relationship to be sullied by any feelings of guilt emanating from a suppressed libido.'

She is a lovely talker, isn't she? They must be very handy with the languages in Lithuania – very handy with the hands, too. Percy is practically going into orbit. I feel so uncouth behaving like this, but then, when you have an action man kit like mine you don't have a lot of alternative. It sort of takes you over.

'Excuse me.' Miss Zonker peels herself away from the front of my body and pulls open a cupboard. Like a shelf-full of imprisoned moggies a bundle of furry rugs bounds into her arms. She tosses them onto the floor at my feet and prods one with her toe. 'Lie down,' she says.

I am very glad of the opportunity to wriggle into a bit of cover because I feel a right nana standing under the arc lights without as much as a dab of athletes foot powder to deaden the shine on my shimmering torso. Down at floor level it is much cosier. That fur feels fantastic against your skin! I do hope it is not habit forming. I would hate to feel that I had to borrow Mum's fox stole next time I felt like a spot of nooky. You would have to watch the teeth, too, wouldn't you?

'That's nice. Face me. Don't smile.' *CLICK!*

She is still taking photographs. I feel like a one hundred-and-eighty pound baby on a tiger skin rug.

'Can you move –? No. A bit more – no. Let me –'

'Ooh!' She certainly knows how to arrange her sitters. *CLICK!* I have only just stopped blinking when she burrows into the furs beside me and snuggles close. 'Now, where were we?' she says. I don't think she really expects an answer because her hands dive deep down below where my legs become one big happy family and start drawing themselves up and up and – ooooooh!

'The massage is the medium,' she murmurs.

'Definitively!' I agree with her.

The camera clicks and I wonder whether to tell her that she has forgotten to turn it off. I don't give it a lot of thought because Wanda Zonker has ways of taking your mind off things.

'Is that nice?' she says.

'Fantastic,' I say. 'Do you want me to do it to you?'

'You can't do it to me,' she says.

'I know. I mean, something like it.'

'All right. Gently now . . . gently. Use your fingers like the tip of an artist's brush . . . aaaaaargh! That's better.'

All the time she is talking her own fingers are doing a spot of hampton courting and I feel that I must express my gratitude in practical terms.

'Aaaah,' she sighs. 'That's heaven. I can see you're becoming less inhibited already.'

I don't say anything because Mum always told me it was rude to speak with your mouth full.

## CHAPTER 2

In which Timmy goes to Beauty Manor and is taken on a revealing tour by Lady Baulkit.

'Centre spread of "Woman Now!"' says Sid sourly. 'All right for some I suppose.'

'I believe they did a lot of retouching,' I say.

'They'd have to, wouldn't they?' sneers Sid.

'On the body hues,' I say. 'Come on, Sidney. There's no need to be like that. Just because I was the first British Mr November in the magazine's history. I had no idea they were going to use the pictures.'

'I can't see why they did it,' moans Sid, looking me up and down. 'There must be hundreds of blokes with better physiques than you. Blokes who have whittled themselves down to a tight knot of whipcord muscle. Blokes like me for instance.'

'I think you may have whittled a bit too far,' I say. 'Wanda told me that she daren't use you in case your dongler got obscured by one of the staple holes.'

Well, I don't want to boast but I have never seen Sid in such a state before. He is practically begging me to ring up birds he has not seen for ten years to prove that there is nothing wrong with his equipment. Of course, I made the whole thing up so I just sit back and enjoy myself. It goes to show how some blokes are always worried that another bastard has got a beauty that plays 'Land Of Hope And Glory' while it submerges. I say 'another' but I reckon that we are all a bit like that. I know I am. The trouble is that you never see the opposition on the rampage, do you? You don't know what you're up against – or rather, what the bird you fancy is, was or has been up against. You see a bit of the placid flaccid when you're in the changing room at the baths but – unless you lead a very exciting private life – it is not often that a male nasty in full flight skims past your peep holes.

I know they say in all those books that size does not matter but if I don't believe it, what chance have you got of convincing a bird? The books have got to say that, haven't they? I mean, you can't spell out the brutal facts too bluntly, can you? Some blokes might decide to knot themselves. It seems obvious to me that a whopperchopper is going to turn a bird on like a good pair of top bollocks do a bloke. Anyway, the point is that Sid is reeling on the ropes and things don't get any better for him when he sees my fan mail. Really! Some of those letters! Talk about 'come up and see me sometime'. It is more like 'drop 'em and cop this!' No finesse at all.

'I am slim, blonde and very adventurous and I would like to make love to you until the cows come home.' Some of the ones from women don't mince the monosyllables either.

'Blooming nut cases!' snorts Sid. 'Nobody in their right mind would want to be mixed up in anything like that.'

'Just wait till I've finished signing these photos,' I say. 'Oh dear, I wish I had a shorter name sometimes.' I raise my hand to my mouth. 'Sorry! I shouldn't have said that.'

'Said what?'

'About being short.'

Sid turns scarlet. 'Will you belt up!? There's nothing wrong with me I tell you.'

Honestly, it is like taking candy from a kid.

Soon after I have been asked if I will stand as a Liberal candidate, Sid leaps round to Scraggs Lane with his face wreathed in smiles.

'It's settled!' he says. 'Wanda has come to an arrangement with Sir Henry. She's been after his seat for a long time.'

This does not come as a complete surprise to me. She did a few funny things when I was with her. Nice but – well – funny.

'I'm very happy for them,' I say.

'Long Hall,' says Sid gazing into the distance.
'Was it?' I say. 'I suppose she wanted time to be certain.'
'What are you blathering about!?' says Sid, unpleasantly. 'I'm talking about Long Hall, Sir Henry's country seat. We're going to turn it into Beauty Manor. Don't you remember anything you're told?'
'It all comes flooding back, now,' I say. 'I've been so busy with the modelling that I haven't had time to keep up. By the way, Sid. When do I get paid for all this?'
Sid waves his hands in the air as if trying to dry them quickly.
'I don't know. You'll have to ask Wanda.'
'But she told me to talk to you about it.'
Sidney closes his eyes. 'Look, Timmo. We've got a lot on our minds at the moment. This health farm thing could be very big. It needs constant attention. You'll get your money. I've never let you down yet, have I?'
'You've never not let me down, Sid. The last time I asked you for some cash you owed me you said "leave it to me, Timmo". That's what I've been doing all my bleeding life, leaving you money!'
This kind of argument makes less impression on Sid than a caterpillar stamping on reinforced concrete but at least it ensures that he takes me with him and Wanda when they go down to Long Hall.
I am quite partial to the country, once you can get to it, and I have a nice game with Wanda seeing who is the first person to spot a cow – it takes us forty miles, and then it is hanging up in the window of a butchers. Sidney is a rotten sport and will not play. I think he is sulking because he did not think of the idea in the first place – though maybe he is still worrying about the size of his dongler. Acornitis is what I have taken to calling his condition. Every time we drive past an oak tree I shake my head and he goes spare.
'Here we are,' says Wanda when we are somewhere on the other side of Henley. 'Turn right at the gates.'
We sail past a couple of stone lions holding shields in

front of their goolies and I soak up the acres of rolling park-land sprinkled with clumps of trees. It is better than any nick or reform school I have ever been to. I never knew you could see places like this if you were not a lunatic or a con. At the end of five hundred tons of gravel is a warm red brick house with two wings and hundreds of windows – looking at them makes me blooming glad that I'm not still in the window cleaning game. You could perish your scrim on that lot.

'This isn't the place, is it?' I say. 'Not all of it?'

'All of it,' breathes Wanda. 'Europe's most modern beauty farm.'

'You can't have bought it?' I say. 'It must be worth millions.'

'We've set up a company which will run the estate as a beauty farm, restaurant and superior country club. In return for our management expertise and a share of the profits from the enterprise –'

'And because Sir Henry Baulkit owes us a favour,' interrupts Sid. 'We have carte blanche to convert the house to meet the requirements of its new usage.'

I can't recall what Carte Blanche looks like but I remember the name. She must be one of those posh interior decorators you read about in the dentist's waiting room.

'Where is Sir Henry going to live?' I ask.

'He has a house in town which he uses when Parliament is sitting. His wife and daughter will be moving into the dower house.'

'What's wrong –?'

'"Dower" spelt D-O-W-E-R not D-I-R-E,' says Sid. 'Spare me the Abbot and Costello routine.'

'No need to be so touchy,' I say. 'You never learn if you don't ask.'

'Can you see that doe?' says Wanda.

'You bet I can,' says Sid. 'We should make a million out of this little caper.'

'I was referring to the deer,' says Wanda coldly.

'Tch, Sidney!' I say. 'You've got a little caper on the mind, haven't you?'

Sidney's reply to my botanical jibe is unnecessarily coarse and hardly suitable for repetition in a book of this kind. I am glad when we arrive at the pillared front door.

'Blimey!' I say. 'Take a gander at that bird. It looks like the hat Aunty Edna wore at Uncle Albert's funeral.' I remember the item well because there was a lot of talk about it at the time in family circles. It was also considered that the choice of scarlet stockings was inconsistent with the impression of a woman trembling on the brink of physical collapse over the loss of a dearly loved one. No one was very surprised when she married the coal man two months later. 'She always had dirty finger nails,' said Gran significantly.

'That's a peacock,' says Sid following my gaze. 'Blimey. Haven't you ever been to Battersea Park?'

'Some bugger nicked them two days before I went,' I say. It is funny, but now that Sid reminds me, I seem to recall that the keeper was reported to have seen a coloured bloke climbing out of the aviary. I suppose it could have been a coal man . . .

'Don't look for a door bell,' says Sid scornfully. 'Houses like this don't have them. Fold your mit round that piece of wire and give it a pull.'

I do as I am told and we are lucky to avoid serious injury when the lightning conductor comes hurtling down and misses us by inches.

'It's going to need a few bob spent on it,' says Sid, wisely.

'What do you think of the weathercock?' says Wanda.

'Not bad for the time of year,' says Sidney. Sometimes I don't know if he is trying to be funny. Before I have the chance to find out the front door opens. An elderly geezer wearing a stained tail coat and a haughty expression looks down his hooter at us.

'We have all the clothes pegs we need,' he says coldly and tries to close the door.

'Hold on a minute, Roughage,' says Sid. 'It's me. Remember? I came round with Sir Henry.'

'I don't even remember the two of you being unconscious,' says the ancient retainer. I can sense that with two such ace gag smiths as him and Sid together sparks are surely going to fly.

'Roughage! Surely you remember me? I'm going to convert the house into a spa.'

'You're wasting your time. There's a new Tescos just down the road.'

'Stop trying to close the door on my foot! Miss Zonker and I have a perfect right to be here.'

'Does she charm warts?' says Roughage, showing faint signs of interest.

'She charms anything,' I say gallantly.

'Shall I show him my credentials?' says Wanda.

'Don't overdo it,' says Sid. 'You can have too much of a good thing.'

'What about fortune telling?' says Lizard Chops. 'Her ladyship has been powerfully attached to the crystal ball in her time.'

'Quality rather than quantity, eh?' says Sid, sounding comforted. 'I don't know where you get the impression that we're gypsies.'

'And don't park your caravans up by the pigs,' says Roughage who seems to be a bit hard of hearing.

'You mean, because of the smell?' says Sid.

'That's right. Two of the pigs passed out last time. We had to give them mouth to mouth resuscitation.'

'How horrible!' says Wanda.

'It was. Both of them died.' Roughage scratches his head thoughtfully. 'Maybe there's something in those toothpaste advertisements.'

'Come, come, my good man,' says Sid. 'We can't stand here talking all day. Miss Zonker and I have work to do.'

'And so have I,' says the grey-haired Roughage. 'I'm supposed to be helping her ladyship move into the dower house. She's very put out by the way things have gone.'

'I'm certain Sir Henry has her interests at heart,' says Sid. 'Timothy, why don't you give Roughage a hand while I help Miss Zonker decide where to put her equipment?' He runs his horny hand up the small of her back and I imagine the evil little thoughts that are pelting through his mind – even an evil little thought likes to keep moving in a place like that.

'Of course,' I say. 'Where shall we meet?'

'Down by the lake,' says Sid. 'There's a gazebo at the far end.'

'He won't still be there when I've finished, will he?' I ask.

'A gazebo is a kind of summer house,' says Sid, as if pronouncing the words causes him pain. 'You'll have to become a lot more araldite if you want to be a success at Beauty Manor.'

'You mean "erudite", Sid,' I tell him. 'Araldite is something you use for sticking parts together.'

'I've never found that necessary, myself,' says the little Lithuanian knocker factory.

'Whatever I mean, you've got to smarten yourself up,' says Sid. 'Everything here has got to be done with tremendous couth.' He does not wait for a reply but scampers off hand in hand with Wanda. Roughage clears his throat and looks round as if for somewhere to spit.

'I don't hold with it myself,' he says. In the weeks to come this is a phrase that falls frequently from his withered lips.

'I suppose we'd better get on with it,' I say.

Roughage looks me up and down with contempt. 'No need to rupture yourself,' he says. 'We've got all day.'

I am about to point out that I have considerably less than all day when the ancient retainer beckons me into a room bigger than anything I have ever seen outside the labour exchange. There are pictures painted all over the walls, and the ceiling looks like the sky with a load of fat tarts lying on clouds and being touched up by cherubs. Quite saucy it is really.

'You don't need a telly, do you?' I say cheerfully.

Roughage looks sourer than a furry yoghourt. 'Them Baulkits wouldn't give you the time of day,' he says. 'They take the batteries for the cook's transistor out of her wages.' Before I can reply he walks over to a long polished table and picks up a cut glass decanter full of booze. Removing the stopper he takes a long swig. This is not easy because the mouth of the decanter is square and I can see why the front of Roughage's suit looks as if it has been used for pressing out the lumps in a vat of treacle.

'Elevenses,' he says with a loud hiccup. 'One of the perks of the job.' He opens the lid of a silver cigarette box and slips his hand inside. 'OW!'

When he has stopped jumping about I help him remove the mouse trap from his fingers and he sticks his digits in his cakehole. It is not a course of action I would have followed myself, but then, I never did reckon that mice were as clean as a bar of Lifebuoy.

'It's no wonder they can't get the servants these days,' he says. 'Who would put up with that kind of treatment when they could be making more money as a toast master?'

'You'd get fed up with making toast all the time,' I say. 'Anyway, the machines are taking over.'

Roughage gives me a funny look and for a moment, I think that he is going to say something. Then he takes another swig from the decanter.

'What is it?' I say.

Roughage smacks his lips together for a couple of moments and then an expression of extreme distaste begins to dawn on his face. 'Syrup of figs!!' he shouts and pushes past me into the hall.

What a funny set-up, I think to myself. His taste buds must be a bit on the dicky side if he can make a mistake like that. I always thought that butlers were supposed to know their way round a bottle of plonk.

It is also clear to me that relations between employer and staff are not going to teach Ted Heath any lessons. Roughage seems to awaken feelings of distrust in the Baulkits and I am not entirely surprised. I would not leave him alone with my money box and a bent hairpin.

'What are you doing here?' I whip round to see a bird of about forty peering at me from the doorway. She is wearing a lot of makeup and a suspicious expression. Although a bit on the thin side she is definitely not undesirable. She plucks anxiously at a string of pearls and feeds a second helping of upper class accent into my lug holes.

'You're not a sex maniac, are you?'

'No,' I say, taken aback.

'Oh.' She sounds disappointed. Knickers! I always have to go and say the wrong thing. 'Then what are you doing here?'

'I'm helping your butler with the move,' I say. 'Are you Lady Baulkit?'

'For my sins,' says the bird fluttering her eyelashes at me. 'That's the best way of marrying into the aristocracy, you know. When I met Henry I was wed to another.'

I nod understandingly. Dad has frequently pointed out to me that the upper classes get away with murder when it comes to sack jumping and make hideous mockery of the nuptial couch. He is dead jealous, of course.

'He was a retired Lieutenant-Colonel in the Pay Corps and we lived in Scotland. I met Henry when he came up for the shooting.'

'Grouse?' I say.

'No, the village post mistress. The role of mistress was one she filled for more than just the G.P.O. Her husband was a very jealous man. Henry was cutting his teeth on the Aberdeen Press and Journal at the time. He always had a penchant for journalism.'

'I expect it came in very handy,' I say, wondering what she is on about. These upper class bints are inclined to be gluttons for the rabbit. I remember from my window cleaning days how they would always be bending your lug holes over a muffin and a cup of jasmin tea.

'It was love at first sight,' she says. 'Rude men have always appealed to me. In those days he would pull his pyjamas on over his riding boots. It took me six months of marriage to stop him wearing spurs in bed.'

I nod my head sympathetically. Fascinating how the other half lives, isn't it? Oh well. Please yourself.

'Does any of this stuff have to be moved?' I say, looking round the room.

'No. If you touched anything it would collapse in a cloud of dust. It's upstairs that I need some help.' She tries to flutter her eyelashes but they carry so much mascara that one set sticks together and falls on the floor. I gaze out of the French windows like a gent while she repairs the damage.

'Are you from the village?' she says.

'No. I'm employed by Inches Limited,' I say. 'You've probably met my brother-in-law, Sidney Noggett?'

'Does he have very cold hands?' she says.

'I don't know,' I say. 'I don't think anyone in the family has ever mentioned it.'

'They're probably used to it,' she says. 'You do get used to things like that. I remember my first husband – just.'

'When you were living in Scotland?' I say, trying to show interest.

'No. Nairobi. Kenneth was my second husband. I met him in Kenya.'

'That's why you pronounce it like that, is it?' I say, keeping the conversation bubbling along.

'No,' she says, coldly. 'I have a friend at the BBC who explained it to me. Anyway, what I was trying to say was that he had very cold hands.'

I am not quite certain whether she means Kenneth, the first husband or the bloke in the BBC. On reflection, it does not seem to matter very much.

'Where is Roughage?' says her ladyship.

'I think he was taken a bit short,' I say, trying to put as good a face on it as I can.

Lady Baulkit picks up the decanter he was glugging from and holds it up to the light. 'I'm not surprised,' she says. 'He's been at the syrup of figs. Ghastly old man. I don't know why Henry keeps him on. Sentiment, I suppose. He's been attached to the family so long we call him verruca.'

I nod understandingly and come to the conclusion that Lady Baulkit has a very nice set of pins. I have never been so close to a titled bint before and the experience sends a nervous tremour through my action man kit. Of course, it is too much to hope for that a spot of in and out might be on the cards but the thought alone is enough to send a warm glow skipping the length of my love portion. You only have to sound all your aitches to make me score heavily on the humble meter.

'Of course, it's not easy for a woman.' Lady Baulkit's voice trembles and she looks deep into my mind – about six inches deep. 'The responsibility of the house and servants. Henry is away most of the time.' She stretches out a hand and touches my wrist. 'A woman has needs.'

'Too true,' I gulp. 'Well, I – er suppose we'd better go upstairs.' I mean, of course, to help with moving her things. I hope she does not misunderstand me. I step towards the door.

'Don't go that way. We'll take a short cut.' Lady B. glides to the fireplace and grabs one of the carved cherubs by his John Thomas. Ouch! – it makes me wince to see her do it. A flick of the wrist and – blimey! A panel beside the fireplace slides open and I can see a flight of stairs.

'In the old days, this is what you had to do to get into the priest's hole,' says her ladyship.

'Really,' I say. It is not a subject I feel keen to pursue. I believe that they had a lot of funny habits in those days.

'There's a network of secret passages connecting most of the rooms in the house,' says Lady B. 'Charles II used to stay here a lot with his lady friends.'

'Very nice, too,' I say. 'Do we need a torch?'

'Just take my hand.' Lady B. grabs my mit before you can say 'Kismet'.

'Blimey! It's dark, isn't it? Are these stairs safe?' The panel has slid shut behind us and my guide laughs lightly.

'That depends who you're with,' she says.

I don't want to jump to any hasty conclusions but a number of things that she has said and done suggest that she may be a bit on the fruity side – like a ton and a half of sultanas, for instance.

Now that we are in what you might call an enclosed space her perfume begins to run riot through my conk and the sound of her silk dress swishing in the darkness awakens what my old headmaster used to call unhealthy thoughts.

'It's rather fascinating,' breathes Lady B. 'There's a number of peep holes along here. You can keep an eye on the staff if you have a mind to.' She pauses so that I nearly bump into her and pulls something aside so that a crack of light appears. 'Look,' she says after a pause. 'Cook is rolling out the pastry.'

I apply my eye to the crack and – blimey! Cook is indeed rolling out the pastry – with the help of Roughage. He has made a remarkable recovery and is performing with no little agility for a man of advanced years. Another dollop of dough drops onto the floor and he kicks it savagely under the table. I must make a point of steering clear of the flap jacks – especially the ones with a seam.

'The staff seem to get on well with each other,' I say, deciding that some comment is probably expected of me.

'Yes. I'm surprised that cook still has it in her.'

'She doesn't any more,' I say, removing my eye from the crack. Short but sweet is probably the best that can be said for Roughage's doughnut filler.

'You have to be so careful with your menials, these days,' murmurs Lady B. 'Rub them up the wrong way and you've got a nasty problem on your hands.'

I feel myself blush scarlet in the darkness. I know we live

in emancipated times but I never like to hear a woman talking like that. It's not nice, is it?

'This is the Seymour Room along here,' she says. 'One of the largest four posters in the country.' She applies one of her mince pies to another peep-hole and gives a sharp exclamation of disgust. 'Well really! They might have taken the counterpane off first.'

I try to get a shufti but she shrugs me aside and flicks open another peep-hole. 'Twin-viewing,' she says. 'It's no fun going to a show by yourself, is it?'

I grunt my thanks and we settle down to take an independent view of the proceedings. My first glance explains to me why they call it the Seymour Room. I have not seen more in a long time. This bird is lying on the bed absolutely starkers and there is some bloke zooming over her contours like a Flymo Lawnmower. I can't see his face, and I don't reckon she can the way he is heading. It is definitely for mature adults and I feel Lady B. stiffen in the darkness. She is not the only thing. Percy gets the message that good times are rolling and starts trying to clamber over the front of my Y-fronts like he is on a Royal Marine Commando assault course.

'Who are they?' breathes Lady B. 'It's bad enough when the house is open to the public without complete strangers –' She stops just as Sidney comes up for air.

'You recognise him, do you?' I say.

'The one with the cold hands! What's he doing here?'

'He's practising giving the kiss of life to a bird who has got a coal scuttle wedged over her nut,' I say.

'Don't be facetious! I mean, why is he here at all?'

'He's siting Miss Zonker's equipment,' I say. 'You must know all about Inches Limited and Beauty Manor. Your husband is one of the directors.'

'He never tells me anything,' she says. 'Our marriage is a marriage in name alone. I'm expected to vacate my home so that perfect strangers can fornicate in it while he cavorts in town. I ask you: is that fair?'

'Not bad,' I say, concentrating on what I can see through the keyhole.

'I've mouthed a few imprecations in my time, I can tell you.' She doesn't mind what she says, does she? I reckoned she might be a nunga nibbler when I first saw her. You can tell, you know. It's something about the way her eyes shine.

'Smashing,' I say. Now Wanda has got on top of Sid and is pinning him down with her arms while she bashes out the theme of Ravel's Bolero on his magic poundabout. It is not exactly the bedrock of children's television but it is absorbing viewing.

Lady B. obviously agrees with me. 'You can imagine how I feel watching that,' she says. I don't have to imagine for long because her hand steals out and draws one of mine to her. She seems to be trembling.

'You feel very nice,' I say.

A fine haze of dust is now falling from the top of the four poster bed and the whole structure is vibrating like a tin shit-house in a hurricane. A grand stand finish is clearly on the cards and one of the pictures on the wall at the end of the room crashes to the floor.

Lady B. groans. 'That's a Van Dyke.'

'He's very versatile, isn't he?' I say. 'Though I didn't think much of his English accent in Mary Poppins.'

Further discussion on matters artistic is denied us because the canopy over the four poster bed collapses in a great cloud of dust and rat shit.

I am not sorry that the sight of Sid on the job has been banished from my eyes because it was getting a bit heavy. Once he turns purple and his eyes glaze over I would rather watch a good horror movie. It is like those Swedish films when they start all that thrashing and moaning. It quite puts me off my cornflakes.

'My God. That's priceless!' yelps Lady B.

'It is a bit funny, isn't it?' I say. 'Especially with his legs sticking out of the end.'

'I meant – oh! It's too awful!' Her voice is almost a

shriek and it is a good job that Sid and Wanda are in a somewhat muffled condition. It would be most unfortunate if their concentration was shattered.

'Supposing we can't get it up?'

She is a very funny woman, this one. There is no doubt about it. Not only forward but pessimistic with it. I think maybe that her mind has become a bit unhinged due to lack of oggins. Because she can't get it she has to try and persuade herself that it wouldn't work anyway. Maybe this is a case for SUPERDICK – yes! I can see it all. Somewhere behind the wainscotting of ancient Long Hall, attractive Lady Baulkit yearns for a spot of in and out like what she can see being dished out in the appropriately named Seymour room. Beside her, simple unaffected Timothy Lea cowers in the darkness and feels the change in his pockets – the change that will turn him into: SUPERDICK!!

'I meant the canopy, of course.'

'Oh.' My expectations drop lower than a newt's knackers. I wish people would make themselves clear. It would save so much disappointment.

'You thought I meant something else, didn't you? Naughty boy!' Suddenly Lady B. is a lot closer than last Christmas and her perfume is holding hands with my aftershave lotion.

'I wasn't certain,' I say.

'It's difficult to remain unmoved, sometimes.' Lady B.'s soft hands rest lightly on my cheeks. 'I think you'd better come to my bedroom.'

She takes a few steps in the darkness and there is a grinding noise. It could well be percy rubbing against the back of my zipper but in fact it is another secret panel. It slides back to reveal a bedroom only slightly smaller than the one Sid was scoring in. Everything is hung with drapes like a Punch and Judy show and your wrist would go limp just looking at it.

'You have a lovely place, here,' I say.

'And you have a lovely place, here,' says her ladyship

with feeling. She obviously doesn't mess about, this one. Once she gets a sniff of the winning post it's ears down and away! 'When you think what is happening around us it seems not entirely inappropriate for us to snatch our own personal moment of happiness.'

'Snatch' seems to be the operative word. I have known some ladies who were quick on the drawers but this little number is leaping out of her threads like somebody has shouted 'abandon slip!' Once again, I get a practical demonstration of how upper class bints strip to the buff without as much as a 'how's your father?' I suppose when you live in a place as big as this you never reckon that anyone is going to come barging through one of the doors.

Her bra and panties have hardly touched the floor before she has wrapped herself around me like an apron and is nibbling at my chest like she is trying to trace a pattern on it. 'It was quite exciting in the passage, wasn't it?' she murmurs. 'Arousing, I suppose is a better word.'

I don't think my action man kit would disagree with her. A half-starved kangaroo couldn't jump higher if you were waving a fresh lettuce under its hooter. Somewhere at the very back of my mind a faint feeling of guilt struggles to the surface. I suppress it. Sir Henry did not look as if he was posing for an election poster in that photograph with the two birds. I might have voted for him if he had been – 'Vote Baulkit for unlimited crumpet'. I reckon that would go down pretty well as a manifesto.

'Have you lost your tongue?' says Lady B.

'Nearly,' I say. 'You've got very deep ear-holes.' Lady B. sighs. 'I was referring to your verbal technique – or rather, lack of it. You are a very silent wooer, are you not? I sense that you would be hard put to plight your troth.'

'I don't know,' I say. 'I can still touch my toes without any trouble.'

Lady B. gives me what Mum would call an old-fashioned look and shakes her head. 'I can see that with you actions must speak louder than words. Very well. Don't be afraid of deafening me.'

It takes me a couple of seconds to work out what she means and by that time she has forced me back onto the bed. With a noise like a box of buttons falling on the floor she wrenches open my shirt and drags her nails down my chest as if hoping to find something underneath them at the end of the trip. No wonder Sir Henry needed professional help. This is a very demanding lady.

'Do you know how long it's been?' she husks.

'Six and one eighth inches,' I say. 'Mind you, I wasn't including that bit they leave on the end of the ruler. It would probably be fairer to say a shade over –'

'I wasn't referring to your private parts,' says Lady B. There is an edge of desperation in her voice that I find hard to understand. 'I was wondering if you could guess how long it was since I last made love?'

This in an interesting question and I try to give it the thought it deserves. It can't have been too long because the fact that she is tearing my trousers off means that she knows roughly the right direction in which to travel. She has not had time to forget everything.

'Search me,' I say. In some ways it is funny that I should use those words because she is turning me over like a customs officer hearing a loud ticking noise coming from a bloke who is not wearing a watch.

'Two months,' she breathes. 'Two months without the solace of the flesh.'

'It doesn't bear thinking about,' I say. I mean it, too. All your washers could perish, couldn't they? This puts a completely different complexion on it as the bishop said when the Nigerian lady gave him a blow job. Now I am practically performing an act of mercy. My own private society for the relief of distressed gentlefolk.

'Hold on a minute,' I say. '– and I don't mean to my hampton. It's not going to go anywhere.'

I am trying to take my socks off, you see, because I hate

looking like a refugee from a dirty photograph – I've been in too many, purely by chance, of course – but this bird is groping me something disgusting. I sympathise with her problem but I don't like people tearing off the lid of the box before the wrapping paper has been removed.

'Steady on!!' I bellow, chucking her back against the bed. She is starkers except for a black choker round the neck and I am starkers except for a pair of nut chokers round the waist pipe. Looking down at her I am reminded of that James Bond book – *From Stockwell With Love*, or something like that and the thought makes me hornier than a herd of rhinos – I was going to say rhinoceroses but it is very difficult to spell and doesn't look right anyway.

Pausing only to remove my Captain Superman Mini-Briefs – no easy task with percy playing space probes – I take off for the bed and make a perfect one point landing. Fortunately, Lady Baulkit's animal eagerness and the fact that she is a needing – as well as a kneading – person has helped to overcome my inborn inferiority complex when it comes to hob-nobbing – or nob-lobbing – with the upper classes.

'Oh! That's heaven!' she squeals. 'You are clever!' She is gazing up to the ceiling of the four poster and a quick crick in the neck shows me that it is covered with panels of reflecting glass – mirrors I believe they are called in some circles. Every aspect of our activity is picked up and thrown back to us. I can see my face quite clearly. It is smiling.

## CHAPTER 3

In which Sidney challenges Timmy to a pentathlon on Clapham Common and a number of distressing things happen.

'You managed to get Miss Zonker's equipment sorted out, did you?' I ask.

Sid shakes his head. 'It was very embarrassing, Timmo.'

'You look a bit flushed, Sid.'

'We'd just gone into this room to see if it would be all right for the Kleinhausen Volcanic Mud Machine when one of the pictures fell off the wall.'

'Just like that?'

'They're all cavity walls, Timmo. The place is probably riddled with secret passages. Anyway, it fell on top of a candlestick and split right down the middle.'

'How unfortunate, Sid.'

'Yeah. That's what I thought. Still, it might have been worse. The picture was on its last legs. I wouldn't have had it in the house. We stuck it up with a bit of sellotape and it's come out quite good really. The bloke looks as if he's got a gap between his teeth but you can't work miracles, can you?'

'Very seldom, Sid. Well, I don't know what you're worrying about. No real harm was done, was it?'

Sid looks grim. 'There's more to tell. We were just tiptoeing out of the room when the bed collapsed.'

'Blimey, Sid! The place sounds like a death trap.'

'Exactly the same thought was occurring to me, Timmo. I think there's a lot to be done before we're ready to receive guests.'

'Where's Wanda?' I ask innocently.

'She's gone back to the car. She was nearly suffocated when the bed fell on her.'

'"Fell on her"!?' I say. 'She was walking across it, was

she?' Sid turns a richer shade of scarlet. 'No, of course not. It just sort of fell all over the place.'

'Really broke up, eh?' I say. 'Split its sides. You must have said something funny, Sid.'

Sid looks disgusted. 'It's nothing to make jokes about. Somebody could have done themself a very nasty injury. I want to have a word with Lady Baulkit about it. You haven't seen her, have you? Tall, skinny bird who really chucks it about. They ought to call this place Come Hither Manor not Beauty Manor. You'll have to watch yourself there, Timmo. She's a raver, that one.'

'I have met her,' I say coldly. 'When I last saw her she said she was going to have a little nap. Things had been getting on top of her.'

'That's nothing new.' Sid watches my face expectantly and nudges me in the ribs. 'Do you get it? "Things getting on top of her". It's a joke.'

If there is one thing I can't stand it is having my own tiny attempts at humour being fed back to me as originals. I am also less than thrilled to think that Lady Baulkit was telling a fib when she said that she had been without a spot of the other for two months. The way Sid goes on she is anyone's for a packet of Woodbines. Even the odious Roughage may have slotted his sprocket.

No sooner has the thought occurred to me than a lady with flour all over her hands runs into the room. 'Lawks a mercy!' she cries. 'Come quickly! Please, gentlemen. Mr Roughage has passed out in the pantry!' Her large, flour-covered arse leads the way out of the door and Sid and I lengthen our strides.

'You see?' says Sid. 'Everything in this place is on the blink.'

* * *

In the weeks that follow I do not see a lot of Sid and Wanda because they are tied up with plans for fitting out Long Hall as Beauty Manor. It is not until the builders have actually started work that Sid invites me round to his flash pad in

Vauxhall. There he lives in some state with my sister Rosie and the fruits of their joyous union, Jason and Jerome Noggett. As nasty a couple of tiny coves as ever tried to send the cat on a space walk from the top of the Post Office Tower. Rosie has more nous than the rest of the family put together and has made a fair slice of bread from boutiques and – more recently – wine bars. These horrible assaults on the British way of life are fair coining in the moola and contribute in no small way to Sidney's inferiority complex – mind you, it is not all complex. He is inferior to boot.

'Sit down, Timmo. Fancy a scotch or something?' says Sid expansively. It is funny, but he is always generous at home, although he will never stick his hand in his pocket when he is in a boozer – if he does, he always get his watch winder caught in the lining until someone else has bought the round.

'No thanks,' I say. 'You don't have a light ale, do you?'

'There's a bottle of wine open.'

'Do us a favour!'

Sid puts on his 'Friends Of The Grape' expression. 'Don't knock it, Timmo. Wine is a great aid to the digestion. A little sip between mouthfuls helps you eat slower.'

'So does a thick lip,' I tell him. 'A pint of bitter and a steak and kidney pudding. That's favourite with me. I don't care whether we're in the Common Market or Brixton Market. I am an Englishman where my taste buds are concerned.'

'Then why are you always noshing one of those Chinese take home meals or a curry?' asks Sid, unkindly.

'Because my Mum's cooking is so diabolical and there aren't any other kinds of restaurant about!' I tell him. Really Sid is as thick as two short wanks sometimes.

'That's a wonderful recommendation for English cooking, isn't it?' storms Sid. 'Your mother can't cook it and nobody wants to eat it!'

When I come to think about it I have to concede that the

stupid prick has a point. There is only one thing that a man of honour can do – change the subject.

'You didn't bring me round here to talk about food,' I say. 'What's the pitch?'

Sid flicks his conk the way Paul Newman did in *The Sting* – I would like to kill the short-sighted bird who once told Sid he looked like the bloke – and settles back against his scruffy leather sofa – really, they should get a cover for it.

'I've been having a chat with Wanda and she reckons that we can make use of you while we're waiting for the building work to be finished.' When Sid says 'make use' he really means 'exploit' but I don't say anything. I like to see him hoisted by his own pederast.

'What did you have in mind, Sid?' I say.

Sid takes a deep breath. 'It would be nice to think that Beauty Manor is going to be the first of its type but this, regrettably, is not the case. It will, of course, be the best, but'–

'Get on with it, Sid,' I say. 'I don't want to buy the bleeding place. You've been watching too many party political broadcasts.'

'We want you to case the competition,' says Sid. 'Nip round to a rival establishment and give us a report so that we can see if we're slipping up on anything.'

'What? Me at a health clinic? What am I going to do there?'

'You're going to get fucking fit for a start off!' snarls Sid. 'Get rid of all that puppy fat. You're no bleeding Charles Atlas, mate. You'd be pushed to hold off the bloke who got sand kicked in his mush.'

What a bleeding cheek! Sid has a belly like someone trying to smuggle a Christmas pudding out of a supermarket. I have seen pregnant dachshunds with better stomach muscles – not many but only because you don't see a lot of pregnant dachshunds about.

'You'd better watch what you're saying, mate,' I snap.

'All this rabbit about my physical condition comes a bit thin from a bloke who has to rest his elbow on the Doctor Barnardos box when he sups his pint.'

'Compared to you I'm bleeding magic, rat knackers,' says my uncouth brother-in-law. 'You want to put your money where your mouth is.'

'What!? And have you trying to kiss it away from me? I should cocoa!'

'Don't try and avoid the issue,' says Sid. 'You know what I'm on about. I am referring to a physical challenge.'

'You mean a punch up?' This comes as something of a surprise to me. Sid is not known as a man of violence – not unless you are small and sickly.

'Don't be so uncouth,' says Sid as if the sound of the words 'punch up' was enough to cause him pain. 'I was referring to athletic pursuits. There's nothing I couldn't beat you at.'

For a moment I can hardly believe my lug holes. Sid must be suffering from severe deadness of the nut. I am years younger than him to start off with, before you take my physique and razor sharp reactions into consideration. The poor sod has not got a chance at anything faster than racing demon.

'You're round the twist, Sid.'

'All right, clever dick. We'll put it to the test. How do you fancy a pentathlon?'

'No thanks, Sid. Cigars always make me cough.'

'Gordon Bennett! It's not a beeding cigar. It's what they have in the Olympic Games. Five events: riding, fencing, pistol shooting, swimming and cross country running.'

I begin to see what Sid is getting at. 'That's all very well, Sid. But we can't ride or fence. And where are you going to get a gun from?'

Sid waggles his finger under my nose. 'Don't try and wriggle out of it, yellow belly. We'll have to adapt. For a start off we can use bikes instead of horses. You can remember how to ride a bike, can you?'

Sid is referring to the time he introduced me to the window cleaning trade and a lot of bad habits. I seem to remember that he was quite powerful on the pedal.

'I'm not carrying a ladder,' I say. You have to be careful with Sid. He is craftier than a wagonload of Brooke Bond advertising.

'Don't start fretting,' sneers Sid. 'Blimey. You're turning white already. It'll be straightforward stuff. Once round the common from outside Clapham South Tube Station. I'll stop off for a pint at The Windmill so you can get a bit of a start.'

'What about the fencing, D'Artagnan?' I say, exercising considerable restraint.

'Darts. We can end up with that at The Highwayman.'

'And the pistol shooting?'

'There's a fair up the common. We can do it there. In fact –' Sidney swipes his thigh in true swash-buckling fashion '– we can do the whole lot in one go!'

'Oh yeah!' I say. 'We swim round the island in the middle of the boating lake, I suppose?'

I am being sarcastical but Sid nods his nut vigorously.

'That's right. I tell you what we'll do: start outside the tube station on our bikes. Down to The Plough and right round the common to the fair. Ten shots on the ·22 range – highest score gets two minutes start swimming round the boating lake. Cross country run to The Highwayman and first bloke to get 301, starting and finishing with a double is the winner!'

'Or a bleeding hospital case!' Of course, I am not worried for myself but Sid is a married man with a wife and two kidneys to support. I would hate to see him snatched away in his running shorts.

'A bit too tough for you, is it, pansy boy?' sneers Sid. 'I knew you'd chicken out when it came to the crunch.'

'I was thinking of you, Sid,' I say.

'Don't you worry about me, mate. I'll be down the boozer telling them how you funked it. Faced with the ultimate test of stamina and skill, Lea revealed himself in his true colours – off white with a long yellow streak down the centre.' That's it! You can push a Lea so far and then – POW! Look out, matey!

'I hope the coroner's got some ink in his pen,' I say. 'A cardiac arrest is the only kind you've never had, isn't it?'

I won't report what is said after that because it might offend the more sensitive of my readers. Suffice to say that it is two angry and embittered – e.g. full of bitter – men who find themselves outside Clapham South Tube Station a few days later. Mum and Dad have been waiting at the finishing line since opening time and, slightly to my surprise, sister Rosie has rolled up to act as starter.

I am less than thrilled to find that Sidney has a flashy racing bike I have never seen before, while mine had two flat tyres up till twenty minutes before the race and is still carrying the 'we will rub it better for you' panel that used to be the slogan of the Noggett Window Cleaning Service.

A lot of the Clapham jet set are pouring out of the tube and I feel a right Charley in my shorts and gym shoes. At least I have white socks and brown legs. Sid has white legs and brown socks.

Rosie leans out of the window of her lime green Renault – it is such a vivid colour, I feel like sucking it sometimes – and wishes us luck. 'Don't do yourselves an injury,' she says. 'If you feel it getting too much for you, give it up. Remember, Timmy's got to be fit enough to go to the health farm.'

'Don't worry about me,' I say. 'You want to trade that frog motor in for an ambulance and follow us round. Sid could be needing you.'

'The time for talking is over, big mouth,' says Sid, grimly. 'Give us the off, Rosie. I'll see you in the boozer in a few minutes.' He drops his head towards his handle bars and flexes his calf muscles like the dedicated athlete he isn't.

'On your – your – what is it, Sid?'

'Marks!' says Sid through gritted teeth.

'There's no need to shout at me!'

'Get on with it!' Sid is still hunched up and I notice that the pannier bag on the back of his bike is open. A leather strap is hanging out of it. On an impulse, I thread the strap through the spokes of the wheel.

'On your marks – get – get – get –'

'Knotted!' shouts Sid. 'For Gawd's sake! Why don't you just say "ready, steady, go"?'

'I want to get it right, that's why. If you start shouting you'll fluster me. Right, I've remembered it now. On your marks! Get set! They're off!'

Well, I don't know about 'they' but Sid is. I would never have done it if I had known. The back wheel goes straight up in the air and he goes over the handle bars and lands on his hooter. It is very fortunate that it is not a more sensitive part of his body.

I am almost tempted to stay behind and give him a hand but you can't afford to be too much of a sportsman these days, can you? Do unto others as they would be unto you, only do it first. I whip off past the giant shelter and have practically got to the traffic lights when the bastards turn red. I look round and there is Sid hurtling towards me. For two pins I would jump the lights but there is a copper staring me straight in the mince pies. He smiles one of those slow smiles that coppers smile because they can't wack you over the nut with their truncheons and I feel Sid bristling beside me.

'You bastard!' he says. 'Look at my knees!'

'They're nice,' I say. 'You're lucky to have a set.'

'I bleeding am after what you did,' snarls Sid. 'Right! You asked for it. No quarter will be given.' And so saying, he swings his foot at my wheel.

'Did you see that?' I say to the copper. 'He kicked me in the spokes.'

'Come here, you,' says the copper, waving a horny digit at Sid.

'But officer –'

'Come here!!'

'Ta, ta, Sid.' The lights change and I go off faster than a jar of warm fish paste. What Sid says is not going to get him in any better with the fuzz and I build up the revs as I power towards The Plough. At this rate it could be all over by the time I get to the fair. It serves Sid right because he should never have landed me with this diabolical bike. What can you do when the handle bars come off – the handle bars come off!!?? I steer right to overtake a milk float and end up making an impression on a raspberry yoghourt. Luckily the milk man is in The Highwayman otherwise he might have got a bit narky when he saw what I did to his grocery products. I am not exactly purring with satisfaction, myself. Somebody has clearly nobbled my bike. I am not one to point the finger without clear evidence BUT! It is clearly that scheming fink Sidney! How low can a man sink without getting fag ends up his hooter?

'That shade of pink suits you, ducky.' Sidney sweeps past and I wipe the yoghourt off my mush with the back of my hand. Dirty swine! I will get him for this. I force my handle-bars back on the bike and pedal in pursuit. It is hopeless. With this crate I am making less impression than John Wayne running for president of the Gay Liberation Front. Much as it goes against the grain I will have to bend the rules a bit. The pond the middle-aged wankers use to sail their model yachts is on the left and if I take a short cut behind the row of Gannex macs and yachting caps – hey! Hang on a minute. Don't I recognise that geezer with the teeth and the shaking shoulders? It can't be – no! – but wait –. He does have a bit of time on his hands these days, doesn't he? What is the name of that yacht? *Morning* –

'What do you think you're doing, then?' I am being addressed by a gentleman wearing a suit of the Clapham equivalent of Lincoln green – Battersea brown. He sports a pork pie hat and what at first glance might be taken for a sword. You could be excused for thinking that it is Robin Hood, especially in the surroundings, but it is in fact one of our common or garden park keepers, or park or garden common keepers, or garden or – anyway, you get the idea. The 'sword' is supposed to be used for picking up pieces of waste paper but it also comes in handy for separating couples who have had a couple of Baby Chams and fallen deeply in love – as I know to my cost.

'Just nipping across to the road,' I say, preparing to push off. Brownjob lays a restraining hand on my handlebars. 'You know the penalty for cycling on the common?'

'Castration?' I say.

Brownjob shakes his head. 'Don't try and be funny with me, laddy. Unless you want to end up in a lot of trouble you get off that bike and walk it over to the road.'

Beyond the far side of the pond I can see Sid belting along like a Tour de France winner. Even if I pedal from here I will not have gained anything.

'Piss off, short arse!' I say. The bloke is about twelve inches taller than I am so the remark is not calculated to get him sending me Valentine cards.

I give a vicious dig at the pedals and prepare to sail away in pursuit of Sid. I should be so lucky! Brownjob is no slouch when it comes to wielding his implement and he jabs it neatly into my rear tyre. There is a sound like audience reaction to Harold Wilson performing a strip-tease at Bournemouth Conservative Club and my back tyre is flatter than Twiggy's kid brother. I narrowly avoid a second jab and cycle away accompanied by a noise like a Centurion tank travelling over cobbles.

Nothing on earth is going to make me catch up with Sid before he gets to the fair and I am knackered to the point of heart failure by the time I hear the whirr of the generators and the blare of pop music. For a second, I think I catch a snatch of *Fourteen Times In Twenty-Two Seconds* but it must be my imagination – either that or somebody elses. You never know, do you?

I fall off my bike and plunge into the fairground. If I had been possessed of any sense I would have recced the joint first but I never thought it would be necessary – next time I will be ready for Sid's underhand tricks. Fortunately, it only takes a couple of minutes to catch up with my shifty brother-in-law. He is propped against a counter and preparing to let fly with what looks like one of the last muzzle loaders in the business. I blunder up to the counter just as he squeezes the trigger and a clay pipe shatters.

'Nice shot,' I say.

'What do you mean "nice shot"? You jogged me, didn't you? I was aiming at the target!'

'You'd never know to look at it. How many shots have you had?'

'Five,' says Sid.

'Six,' says the bloke behind the counter. 'He's got one outer.'

'You belt up,' says Sid. 'I'm having that one again. He jogged me.'

If Sid is this lousy a shot I am not prepared to make an issue of it. Blimey, the target is only about twenty feet away.

'Ten shots, please, mate,' I say.

I slide one up the spout, settle to my aim and realise how knackered I am. The end of the rifle is swinging around like a surrender flag. I can't keep my hands still. This is ridiculous. And me a fully paid up member of Her Majesty's mob. Trained to go to vividly exciting places and kill people. My old sergeant-major would turn in his grave. BANG!

I haven't pulled the trigger yet but a neat little hole has appeared in the middle of my target. Thank you, Sid! I squeeze one off as my gun wavers in the direction of the target but I can't see a hole anywhere. Sid's target is still unmarked.

'Do you want to go on, Sid?' I ask, waving at my target. 'I've beaten you already.'

'Fluke,' he says. 'You wait till I've had the rest of my shots.' I let him settle in to his aim and then give the counter a little nudge as I see his finger tightening round the trigger. BANG!

'Right!' says Sid. 'I'm having that again.'

'I wouldn't if I were you, mate,' says the bloke behind the counter. 'It's a bullseye.'

'Cheats never prosper,' says Sid all pious-like. Honestly, I could belt him.

'Are you two, boy scouts?' says the bloke who runs the range leaning forward to take a gander at Sidney's shorts.

'Do me a favour,' says Sid. 'We're bleeding athletes, aren't we?' He squeezes off another shot and one of the coloured light bulbs at the back of the booth shatters.

For a few moments after that, I think that boxing is going to be added to our list of competitive sports. The bloke behind the counter reckons that Sid shot the bulb on purpose and Sid does not want to let on that it was a lousy shot because it will count against his score.

While they argue the toss I try to get my breath back, but I still can't stop my hands shaking. I try five shots and I don't hit the target once. For two pins I would substitute one of the many used targets that our lying around but Sid is watching me like a hawk and I dare not risk it.

I concentrate fit to bust but at the end of my ten shots I have a splitting headache, one bull, one magpie and one outer. It is pathetic but at least it is better than Sid, he still has the one bull I gave him and an outer.

'Right,' I say. 'So that's two minutes start in the swimming.'

'Yes,' says Sid. 'And don't let's have any cheating. You stay put until it's time for you to go.'

'What are you rabbiting on about?' I say. 'I'm going first. I got a better score than you.'

'Bollocks!' says Sid coarsely. 'Two bulls and an outer counts higher than your three.'

'One bull!!' I say, snatching up the target. 'Look! There's one hole.'

'Yea, but look at the shape of it. There's two bullets been through there. It stands to reason.'

There is in fact a slight tear at the edge of the hole but

only a real villain would dare to suggest that it was made by a second bullet. Unfortunately, Sid is a real villain.

'Marvellous bleeding coincidence, isn't it?' I say. 'The whole target with hardly a mark on it and two bullets have to go through the same hole.'

'I'm glad you accept it in that spirit,' says Sid. 'Right. That's two events out of the way and I think that there can be little doubt that I am clearly in the lead.'

'It's first to 301, Mary Peters,' I remind him. 'You save your breath. I haven't begun to try yet.'

A few more words are exchanged on the way to the boating lake and Sid pushes angrily past the pay-box and strides to the end of the jetty.

'Are you paying, mate?' says the bloke behind the pigeon hole. 'You'd better tell Francis Chichester we've only got paddle boats left. The rowing boat has got a rotten bottom.'

'He's just found that out,' I say.

Honestly, I don't know why Sid wanted to step into it. Trying to make a few more inches before he had to start swimming, I suppose.

'You stay where you are!' he bellows. 'Don't try and take advantage.'

I help the daft sod out and he stands shivering in front of me.

'I want you to promise that you won't go until you've counted to a hundred and twenty, slowly,' he says.

'But Sid – !'

'No buts. You don't move an inch until you've finished counting. Right?'

'Right, Sid.'

Sid crouched in a diving position and the bloke comes out of his office. 'You can't swim here!' he says. 'Can't you read the notices?'

'Not without my glasses,' I say. 'I always take them off when I go swimming.'

Sid dives in and immediately he hits the water I start counting: 'One, two, three –'

Sid surfaces about three feet away. He is covered in mud and there is a litter basket wedged over his nut.

'Twenty-two, twenty-three, twenty-four –'

'Help, help!' screams Sid. 'I'm blinded. I can't see!'

'Forty-eight, forty-nine, fifty –'

'Don't just stand there! I'm injured.'

It is not surprising really. Sid has dived into about fourteen inches of water.

'Ninety, ninety-one, ninety-two –'

'Help!'

'– a hundred and eighteen, hundred and nineteen, hundred and twenty. Right, I'm going now, Sid.' I lower myself into the water and wade past him. By the cringe, but it is cold! Muddy, too. 'You don't want to hang about, Sid. You'll catch your death.'

Sid says something but I do not catch his exact words because I have launched myself into the water. Whatever it was, he was definitely not reading a good luck telegram from the Queen.

I take a deep breath and strike out in a powerful crawl. My middle name is modesty but anybody who frequents the Tooting Bec baths trying to pick up the totty stretched out round the fountain will tell you that I am an ace swimmer. Poor old Sid has not got a chance – or rather, he would not have if it wasn't for the weed. The stuff jams the pond like green slimy cotton wool. The fish must have legs to get around. Half a dozen strokes and I come to a dead halt. I must look like Irish night at the Turkish baths.

I look round to see how Sid is getting on but there is no sign of him. He has probably chucked it in. I can't say I blame him either. Some of the things that are floating on top of the weed don't bear thinking about. It makes you wonder what they get up to in those boats.

'Are you all right, mate?' I am being addressed by a bloke who is rowing his bird round the lake – well, it's good to know that somebody is.

'Yes, thanks,' I lie to him.

'Just thought you might need a tow like your mate.'

I follow the jerk of his finger and there is two-timing Sid disappearing round the back of the island. He is clinging to the side of a paddle boat. What a diabolical liberty!

'Follow that boat!' I grab hold of the piece of cord hanging over the back of the dinghy and pull the tart's hand bag into the water. It is a pity that it is open at the time but fortunately most of the stuff gets held up by the weed. She only loses her lipstick, compact, front door key and a few other things like that. I have a grope about on the bed of the lake but all I come up with is a bottle of Guinness which she says was not hers anyway.

By the time we set off in pursuit Sid has got an enormous lead and my bloke has lost a lot of interest. It is the tart's fault. She keeps having a go at him as if I am not there. Blimey! Anybody would think I wanted to chuck her rotten bag in the drink.

In the end the weed clears a bit and I push on by myself. A few fishermen start having a go at me for disturbing their lines but I tell them what they can do with themselves, no trouble. By the time I see the jetty I am knackered fit to bust. Sid is just scrambling out and I recognise Douglas Fairbanks Junior as being amongst the crowd of well-wishers waiting to cheer us ashore. The brim of his brown pork pie hat is trembling and I am glad that he has Sid to cut his teeth on.

'Take your hands off me!' I hear my rotten brother-in-law saying. 'You don't own the park, mate. You're looking after it for the people.'

It occurs to me that it might be as well to avoid the official reception and I start to wade ashore.

'You're coming with me my lad. We'll see what the police have to say about you.'

'Why don't you push off back to your little house? The three bears must be wondering what's happened to you.'

Relations between Sid and the park keeper are definitely becoming strained and it is no surprise to hear angry shouts followed by a loud splash. The crowd parts and Sid can be seen legging it towards The Highwayman. He is definitely game, you have to give him that.

I am watching him admiringly when it occurs to me that I had better get my finger out and set off in pursuit. It is easier thought than done. I can hardly put one foot in front of the other. For a second I flirt with the idea of taking Rosie's advice and chucking it in but I can't bear to think of Sid putting one over on me. If he wins I will never hear the end of it. Summoning my last resources of athletic cliché, I prepare to finish the race of the century.

Sidney is fifty yards ahead of me as we leave the belt of trees round the boating lake and head out across the common. There are about eight hundred yards to go to the boozer but they might be miles as far as I am concerned. The stitch in my side is the only thing that is holding me together. Sidney's little legs are whirring away in front of me and I stumble after him through the twilight and the courting couples settling down to try and make a go of it. Clapham Common is a very romantic place in late summer as any member of the vice squad will tell you.

People shrink away from me in horror and I suppose I must look a bit funny with all the weed draped over me. Not the kind of thing you want to see when you are waiting to take your best girl behind the changing rooms. It could rob the moment of all its magic.

Ahead of me, Sid seems a little closer and I switch my imagination into overdrive in order to close the gap even further: 'Into the blazing crucible of sound that was the Adolf Hitler stadium strode the seemingly invincible Nazi superman, Sidney Noggetheimer. The crowd rose as one but the roar died in their throats. Eating up the space between the two runners was the unheard of young Englishman who up till that morning had been employed as the British team's baggage attendant. Gritting his teeth for one muscle-grinding effort Lea drove his frail frame forward. Sensing the crowd's silence, ex-concentration camp super-fuhrer Noggetheimer turned his bullet-like head. At that moment the race was over. In an instant, Lea was through the gap and –'

''Ere! Watch where you're going, you daft sod!' I have been baulked by one of the runners I have lapped – or rather, a nut salesman replenishing his wares from the back of a van.

'You want to watch your nuts!' I say.

This is a harmless enough remark but for some reason the bloke standing knee deep in 'Fresh Roasted' seems to take exception to it.

'You want to watch your nuts, and all!!' he says menacingly. 'Especially poncing about like that. You a fairy or something, are you?'

'I'm in a hurry,' I say. 'Get out of the bleeding way.'

'Pick 'em up!'

'Sod off!'

'Look, mate. You burst my nut bags.'

'That's going to be the least of your problems,' I say, giving the bloke a little heave.

Oh dear! People are so short-tempered these days. Everyone living off their nerves. Would you believe that the bloke tries to clobber me with his basket? Very nasty it is. I have to belt him one before I can get after Sid.

Of course, the bugger has disappeared and I can imagine him lobbing the arrows into the cork, no bother. I hope Dad is there to see fair play. If he isn't, or if he is too pissed to notice anything, Sid will cheat. There is no doubt about it. I steam round the corner of the boozer and nearly run into a knot of blokes grouped round the cellar hatch.

'Poor bastard,' says one of them.

'He's moving,' says another.

I push my way between them and look down into the cellar. Sid shakes his head and thoughtfully shoves a bottle of lager into the pocket of his shorts. 'Stupid buggers,' he says. He stretches out an arm and starts to haul himself up the ladder. What courage! What tenacity of purpose! I am still marvelling at it as I flash through the door of the boozer and shout for some darts. The geezer behind the bar takes one look at me and puts his hand over the till.

'I can't serve you like that!' he says.

'What's the matter?' I say. 'I've been out for a run, haven't I?'

'You're soaking wet,' he says. 'You're dripping all over the pile!'

I should have known that with The Highwayman all tarted up it was the wrong place to come.

'Give us a pint of cooking and the darts, there's a mate,' I say, patiently. I've got a bet on, see?'

'We don't have any darts,' says the geezer. 'We haven't had any darts since the new management took over.'

Sid crashes through the door and looks round the room. 'Give us those bleeding darts!'

'They don't have any darts, Sid.'

'You're dropping weed all over the carpet,' says the bloke behind the bar.'

'Oh, I say, how absolutely frightful!' Sid swallows his lower lip and puts one hand on his hips while he tips an imaginary hat over his eyes with the other. 'Listen, mate. You hand over those darts or I'll smash your face in.'

'I'm going to have to ask you to leave,' says the barman, turning white.

'Oh, there you are,' says Dad, coming into the bar. 'We were in the garden. The geezer said we couldn't go out there unless we had a kiddy. I told him that I didn't mind trying but I reckoned that we'd left it too late. That's right, isn't it, mother?' Dad shudders with laughter while Mum shudders.

'I didn't know what to do with myself,' she sniffs. 'It's nice here, though, isn't it? Lovely toilets. The soap smelled nice but I couldn't get no lather out of it.'

'Gordon Bennett!' snorts Dad. 'That was the air freshener, wasn't it? Where the bleeding hell did you find it?'

'Ooh!' says Mum. 'I thought they put it there so you'd see it.'

'If you don't withdraw I'm going to call the police,' says the barman.

'We'll go when we're ready,' says Dad. 'I used to come to this place when it was a pub. I might have known when they moved the karsi inside the building the writing was on the wall.'

'The writing was on the wall when it was outside as well,' says Sid.

'What have you two been up to?' says Mum. 'You don't look well. You want to get out of those wet things.'

'I want to finish the pentathlon first,' says Sid grimly. 'I've got this little bleeder reeling.'

'He loosened the handlebars on my bike.'

'He left me to drown!'

'I'm ringing the police,' says the barman.

'You leave that phone alone,' says Dad.

'Blimey!' says a bloke who has just come in. 'Get a load of that, Charley. The monsters from the Green Lagoon.'

'They must have dredged the lake, Fred.'

'Shut your mouth, Grease Bonce!' snaps Sid.

'You try and shut it, Frog Features!'

Well, I have to confess that Sid has a good try. If he doesn't exactly close the bloke's trap he damn near gets his fist wedged in his cakehole. The geezer reels back against the bar and within seconds everybody in the place is having a go at each other. Mum is zapping Grease Bonce's mate over the nut with her handbag and from the effect she is having you would reckon her to be carrying a spare parts kit for steam rollers in the article. Dad is bashing some geezer with the Dr Barnardo's box – until it splits open – when he starts collecting the takings in his cap. Sid is having a go at anybody and I am just prancing about and keeping out of trouble.

At least, I am keeping out of trouble until the door bursts open and the copper who stopped Sid, the park keeper, the nut salesman and about half a dozen people I have not been introduced to bundle into the boozer.

'That's them!' says the park keeper.

'You're dead right it is, mate!' says Dad and belts him straight in the chops.

Something tells me that it is going to be a long evening.

## CHAPTER 4

In which Timmy goes to spy on Bosky Dell Health Clinic and suffers deprivation before being offered succour by warm-hearted Mrs Chalfont.

'The family that slays together, stays together. That's what they say, isn't it?' says Dad.

'Not to the beak, they don't,' I tell the stupid old git. 'Not unless they want to get lumbered with being bound over and fined a hundred quid.'

'The family that stays together slays each other, more like,' says Sid.

'I thought a bit of family solidarity would go down all right in this day and age,' says Dad.

'Yeah. Right down the staircase to the cells. That's where it nearly took us,' says Sid. 'I thought he was going to have a heart attack when you said that.'

'He didn't have a heart, that was his trouble,' says Dad. 'He was a man without feeling.'

'It wouldn't have been so bad if all that Doctor Barnardo's money hadn't have fallen out of your cap when we were being charged,' groans Sid.

'I was only looking after it, wasn't I?' says Dad. 'I wouldn't steal from little orphan kiddies, would I?'

'I don't know so much,' I say. 'Mum said that when she used to be able to get the free orange juice you were always knocking it back. She even said that when she was breast feeding you'd have a go at her if you'd been on the booze the night before.'

Sid covers his face with his hands. 'Don't!' he groans. 'That's about the most disgusting thing I've ever heard.'

'I used to take my teeth out first,' says Dad. Sid leaves the room hurriedly.

It is about a week after the spot of unpleasantness at the

Highwayman that Sid informs me that I am bound for Bosky Dell Health Centre.

'I'm told that it's a lovely setting,' he says. 'Make the most of it and don't forget why you're there. Make a note of everything that happens and keep all the bumf they give you. Bosky Dell is one of the most expensive health farms in the country. If we can match up to their operation, we're laughing.' I notice that he does not say anything about getting fit. The subject has not been mentioned since the pentathlon. Hardly surprising since Sid pulled so many muscles – well, he calls them muscles – that he has been hobbling about with a walking stick ever since.

Sid tells me that I am going to be met at the station and I am really chuffed when I see this geezer in a chauffeur's uniform with Bosky Dell embroidered on one of the lapels. I walk towards him but he looks straight past me and concentrates on a well-stacked bird of about thirty-five carrying a Yorkshire terrier. Mind you – I would have concentrated on her if I had been given the choice.

'Good afternon, Baines,' says the bird.

'Good afternoon, Mrs Chalfont,' says the chauffeur. 'A pleasure to have you back with us again.'

'Thank you, Baines,' says the bird. 'Suky, say hello to Mr Baines.'

'Woof! Woof!' goes the hairy little horror.

Baines tries to adjust his features into a 'welcome, doggy' expression but he obviously finds it an effort. He does not look like a dog lover. On closer inspection he does not look as if he has a lot of affection to spare for anyone.

'Excuse me,' I say. 'I'm for Bosky Dell as well. Timothy Lea.'

'How delightful,' says Mrs Chalfont.

Baines looks at my Chelsea F.C. hold-all as if he prefers pigskin. I do not fear his glance because I have made a big effort to posh myself up and am looking decidedly tasty in my genuine imitation leather jacket and tartan trousers. Quiet but authoritative.

'Is that all you've got?' he says coldly. He is looking at the front of my trousers when he says it and for a moment I wonder what he is on about. Then I realise that he is talking about my luggage.

'We only need a dressing gown and a pair of bathing trunks, don't we?' I ask.

'You are a spartan, aren't you?' says Mrs Chalfont warmly.

'Actually, I'm a Scorpio,' I say.

'Really? How fascinating!' Mrs Chalfont takes my arm and steers me towards the barrier. 'You must tell me all about it. I'm obsessed by horoscopes.' She turns to Baines. 'My luggage is on the trolley.'

'Is that all yours?' I say. I mean, there are about half a dozen bleeding great suitcases.

'One must have something to slip into,' she says. 'After all, I am a woman.'

After all what? I think to myself. I would never have questioned the fact that she was a woman.

'I hope I've got enough,' I say.

'So do I, darling.' Mrs Chalfont squeezes the inside of my arm in friendly fashion. 'Is this your first time here?'

'Yes,' I say. 'I had a friend who told me about it.'

'You're not in the pop business, are you?' she says. 'There's an awful lot of show biz personalities come down here. A de-coke, that's what they call it.'

'Not any more,' I say. 'I used to have a finger in a group, but I've washed my hands of them now.'

'I'm not surprised, darling.' Mrs Chalfont rolls her eyes and sails out of the station entrance. 'The Rolls, Baines?'

'Yes, Mrs Chalfont.'

They do themselves all right at Bosky Dell, there is no doubt about it. I can understand why Sid was moaning about the cost of sending me to the place. You lose a few pounds in more ways than one.

Mrs Chalfont rabbits on cheerfully as we purr through thickly wooded country and I wonder why Christmas trees cost so much. I have never seen so many of the bastards. I learn that Mrs C. comes three times a year – to Bosky Dell, I mean – and uses her two weeks to get in shape to tackle all the booze and nosh that led her to go there in the first place.

'I'd never have the strength of will to do it by myself,' she says. 'I like meeting people, as well. It's easier to be firm if you're doing it with other people, don't you think?'

'Definitely,' I say.

'I expect I'll see more of you once we get there.' She runs her hand lightly up my arm. 'I think you'll like the atmosphere.'

What a friendly lady, I think to myself. I am not surprised to learn that her old man is in public relations.

Bosky Dell looks as if a lot of little houses have grouped together to resist attack from a golf course. It is all different heights and styles of architecture. Big though. I notice a bloke sitting in the middle of a bush eating a packet of biscuits but he throws them over his shoulder when he sees the car coming. I think of mentioning it to Mrs Chalfont but she is so busy telling me how all her inhibitions fly away by the second week that I don't like to interrupt her. The Rolls crunches to a halt outside the main entrance and Baines nearly wrenches my arm off as I try to open the door. I don't know why he should be so narky, I was only trying to help.

'I do hope I've got my usual room,' says Mrs C. 'Number Three, overlooking the lake.'

'Lucky for some,' I say brightly.

Mrs C. narrows her eyes. 'Y-e-e-s.'

We go through the front door with Baines staggering under the weight of the cases and there, sitting behind a desk with a blooming great bunch of flowers on it, is a right little cracker. Just in case you thought she was an out-of-work slaughterhouse attendant she has a sign in front of her saying 'Sheila Winsome, Receptionist'.

'Mrs Chee-alfont! How lee-ovely to see yee-ou!' Miss

Winsome's accent makes Isobel Barnet sound like Henry Cooper with a bad head cold and I get a second helping of the idea that Bosky Dell is strictly for the nobs. This is obviously the impression that is meant to be conveyed because all the fixtures and fittings are the type that makes you wish you had packed your screwdriver, and there is no stinting on the wall to wall carpeting and scrubbed pine.

'I see you've brought your lee-tle free-end with you.'

'Timothy Lea,' I say, 'Actually, we met at the station.'

Miss Winsome looks at me as if I have suddenly appeared beside a bad smell. 'I was referring to the lee-tle dee-og,' she says. 'Are you see-aying the-at you hee-ave a reservation he-ere?' She says it like she is giving me a chance to change my story. Luckily I have been cross-examined by experts.

'That's right,' I say.

'Oh yes.' She overdoes the surprise a bit. 'Room Four. Overlooking the lake. Your consultation will be with Doctor Tensor, after dinner.'

'What a coincidence,' murmurs Mrs Chalfont as we are led down a long corridor. 'Next door neighbours. I hope my furry little friend doesn't keep you awake.'

I am about to say that I would not begrudge a second of the time my eyes were open, when I realise that she is talking about her dog.

'I'm certain she'll be good as gold,' I say stretching out my hand and then whipping it away again as the little monster tries to sink its pirhana fangs into my fingers.

'Naughty Suky!' scolds Mrs C. 'She knows she's not really supposed to be here and that makes her upset. She's very sensitive.'

'What happens at the consultation?' I ask.

'Doctor Tensor will discuss your case history with you and agree whether any particular course of treatment should be prescribed.' She looks me up and down. 'I don't think you're going to have any problems. You look fitter than most people do when they've finished a month's course.'

'I think you're looking in pretty good shape yourself,' I say.

'Too much shape,' says Mrs C. rubbing an envied hand over her chest. 'A bit Junoesque, don't you think?'

'I don't know,' I say thoughtfully. It is easy for me to say that because I don't know what Junoesque means. I do know that Mrs C. has a pair of knockers that look about as welcoming as a turned down counterpane – soft, white and curvy. I could fall asleep on that lot, no trouble.

'Do we have to wear anything special for supper?' I ask.

'Some people dress up a bit,' says Mrs Chalfont. 'But I wouldn't bother. You're probably all right like that.'

I blooming well hope so because I don't have anything else! Gordon Bennett. I thought I was coming on an Outward Bound course, not an ocean cruise.

I lay out my tooth brush and my pyjamas – I thought I'd posh it up while I was away – swill some after-shave down the front of my jockey briefs and I am ready for supper. Mrs C. presumably has more to do because there is no sign of her when I go past her room. Just the hum of something which I take to be an electric toothbrush.

I am feeling a bit apprehended and the sight of the dining room does nothing to cheer me up. It is posher than Aunty Edna's wedding reception where everyone had a serviette you could blow your nose on – Dad did. Some of the geezers are wearing dinner jackets, and they are not even waiters! As for the birds – well, they are really something. I remember seeing a fashion show at Arding and Hobbs when I was on my way to nick a few records and these bints are wearing the same kind of clobber – mind you, it is covering a much larger acreage. Long black numbers with tassels and fringes – they look like expensive lamp shades. And talking about shades – you need a pair to protect your mince pies from the glare of the jewellery. It is like walking round a corner and bumping into Liberace.

Everybody takes a gander at me and I settle down at a table as far away from the others as possible.

'Excuse me, sir. Would you mind sitting at one of the tables that has been laid? This is the serving table.'

I stand up hurriedly and bash my knees against the flap. I should have noticed that there was nothing on the table except a cloth. I find another table and wish that everybody would stop looking at me. To give myself something to do I pick up a fork and start cleaning my nails with it. There is so much cutlery on the table that you could arm an emergent nation with it. At least I am going to get some decent nosh. I am prepared to put up with a lot if it means a change from my Mum's grub. She has the same effect on the lining of your stomach as an oven scourer has on an oven.

'Here we are, sir.'

The waiter geezer slaps down an enormous tureen and my mouth starts watering. I wonder which fork I should use first? The waiter whips off the lid and – blimey! I don't need a fork, I need a microscope. I am staring at what looks like a turnip shaving.

'Hang on a minute!' I say. 'Where's the rest of it?'

'The rest of it?' The waiter looks at me as if I am daft.

'Yeah. The meat and all that. What is this? Some kind of horse's duvet?'

The waiter's lip curls contemptuously. 'An hors d'oeuvres? No, sir. That is your evening meal. Par-boiled turnip. We have a light evening meal here, sir.'

'Light?' I say. 'I've only got to sneeze and I've blown it up my sleeve.'

The waiter tries to look sympathetic. 'It's rich in vitamin C,' he says.

'You're not telling me that's all I get?' If this is a 'light' meal, I wonder what happens when they put you on a diet? Cut bits off you, I suppose.

'You can have the Bosky Dell Compote, sir. It's produced on the premises.'

How disgusting! I suppose Doctor Tensor is known as the Lord of the Manure instead of the Lord of the Manor. No wonder this caper appeals to Sid so much. If what I have been served is a sample meal, a week's catering could be handled out of a tin of diced carrots. I take a shufti round the surrounding tables and most of the nosh gets lost against the pattern on the plate. I can't stand this for two weeks!

'What about something to drink?' I say.

'Certainly, sir. There's monks' water.'

'Oh yes.' After the compote I am not exactly itching for a goblet-full. 'What's that when it's at home?'

'It comes from the Cistercians, sir.'

I might have guessed! If they think I am going to drink a lot of crushed up flowers they have another think coming.

'Forget it,' I say. 'I suppose it's all right if I linger over my turnip! I'd like to savour each delicious mouthful.' When I think about it, I can understand what the bloke was doing in the bushes with his carton of biscuits. I wonder where he got them from? Maybe they were hidden in a parcel of files. I go next door to the library and settle down in front of the TV. Maybe this will take my mind off my stomach. At the moment there is nothing separating them.

'. . . and now Jimmy is going to squirt cream all over my pastry cases.'

Blooming Heck! It would have to be Fanny Raddled, wouldn't it?

'Oh dear. Jimmy's dropped his monocle in the sponge filling. Silly Jimmy!'

I turn the set off quickly. That bird never gives me an appetite at the best of times.

I pick up a copy of *Beautiful Homemaking* and – by the cringe! It would have to flop open at Pineapple Upside Down Paradise Pudding – and in glorious technicolour too. It is all I can do to stop myself from licking the pages. It is sadistic to leave a thing like that lying about. I am so upset that I draw a moustache on Evelyn Home's photograph. Once I have done that it is but a short step to writing in speech captions to all the photographs and half an hour passes more or less agreeably until it is time for me to see Doctor Tensor.

I am not looking forward to the interview because I seldom find that doctors and I speak the same language. This is particularly true in the case of Doctor Ahkmed our local G.P. He does not speak the same language as anybody outside Sholapur. I tap on the door with 'Doctor Tensor' written on it in gold lettering and wait respectfully. There is a rustling noise and a muttered curse before the door opens and Miss Winsome comes out smoothing down the front of her dress. She looks at me with ill-concealed dislike.

'Right-o, Miss Welch. Take your knickers off and lie down on that couch.'

I look away from Miss Winsome towards the owner of the voice. He has a bald head and very hairy arms sticking out of a short-sleeved white tunic. What at first I think is a stethoscope turns out to be a catapault slotted in his top pocket.

'Yerwhat?' I say.

'Just a bit of wish fulfilment,' says the geezer. 'I'm only human, aren't I? If you had a load of fat old gits filing in here and scuffing the edge of your desk with their bellies you'd fancy a change sometimes.'

'Doctor Tensor?' I ask.

'That's right, mate.' Tensor picks up a paper clip and stealthily removes his catapult from his pocket. 'See how the bugger shifted, the minute I got my equaliser out? They're dead crafty, you know.' He nods towards the window and I see that he is referring to a large bluebottle. 'Hang on a minute. Just give him time to settle.'

The bluebottle starts rubbing its hind legs together and Doctor Tensor takes careful aim. Zink! The paper clip misses by half an inch and the bluebottle takes off for the panelling which covers the walls of the room.

'Bugger!' says Doctor T. 'Change of weapons.'

He picks up a length of brass piping and inserts a needle wrapped with cotton waste in one end.

'You are Doctor Tensor?' I ask.

Baldilocks pauses with his blowpipe half way to his lips.

'That's right mate. Don't let the bedside manner fool you.' He puffs out his cheeks and the bluebottle is pinned to the panelling as if on a specimen board. 'Bleeding classic!'

'Very good,' I say.

'Ta,' says the great man. 'I don't usually do so good when I'm being watched. Nothing wrong with you, is there? Just down here for a skive?'

I nod.

'That's good. I hate sick people. It's amazing how many of them there are about.' Doctor Tensor opens a drawer and produces a tumbler and a bottle of Martell cognac which he swiftly introduces to each other. 'Cheers!'

'Cheers,' I say, watching him light a cigar.

'I'd like to offer you a snort, mate. But it wouldn't be right, would it? You're here to refurbish your natural life force, aren't you? To purge yourself of those deadly toxins which threaten to undermine your vitality.' He starts to laugh helplessly. 'It's a blooming carve-up, isn't it? I tell you what, mate. It isn't half doing me a lot of good.'

He puts his feet up on the desk and looks around for more bluebottles. 'I know what you're thinking,' he says, after a pause. 'You're thinking "How does this coarse, uncouth Charley get to run a posh set-up like Bosky Dell?" Well, I'll tell you. When I qualified I realised I wasn't cut out for Harley Street. I didn't need a bleeding crystal ball to find that out. I wasn't what you might call "polished" enough. I'm a no-messing, straightforward sort of geezer so I had to make the most of it. I found that people didn't want to have all that soft soap. The nicer you were to them, the more they reckoned they were dying and you were trying to keep something from them. They also reckoned that if you were rude to them you must know your job otherwise you would never dare talk like that. I get some bloke in here and I say: "Listen, Fatso. You go on stuffing your gut and getting boozed out of your mind you're going to snuff it, never mind about the fags", and he falls on his knees in gratitude. Nobody's ever talked to him like that before. They think I care, you see.'

'But you do care, don't you?' I ask.

'Of course I bleeding care! If they snuff it, they don't come back again, do they? I like to get all my patients just fit enough to last a couple of months before it's time to come back here again. "Health Junkies" that's what I call them. Once they've had a spot of the underwater massage they're hooked.'

'Underwater massage?' I say.

'I reckon it's favourite. Especially with Gretchen checking that she's got the wrinkles out of your gonads. Some people prefer the steam cabinets but it always makes me think of suet puddings – in fact most of the bleeders around here make me think of suet puddings.'

I wish he had not mentioned suet puddings. I could eat one through Dad's vest.

'Hungry, are you?' says Doctor Tensor understandingly. 'It's always worse at first. By next week when your tongue starts to swell you'll hardly be able to swallow your wafer.'

'My wafer?' I say.

'Yeah, that's your Sunday lunch. We used to have blokes who doubled their calorie intake by going to Holy Communion. Terrible it was. We had one bright spark who refused to let go of the chalice. Very nasty.'

'Isn't there any way of getting more food?' I ask.

Doctor Tensor shakes his head and opens another drawer. 'Not unless you resort to the black market,' he says, throwing a packet of biscuits on the table. 'Do you fancy your nuts ginger?'

'How much do they go for?' I say.

'A quid to you. I'll see the bloke gets the money.'

'This is ridiculous!' I say. 'This place costs about a hundred quid a week and people are so hungry they're prepared to pay a quid for a packet of biscuits!'

'Two quid. I was making you a special offer because I

liked your face. Ah well, just a thought. You never had any heart attacks, have you?'

'Not yet.'

'Good. Then you should be all right on most of the toys. Don't start fiddling with any of the switches. We had a bloke last week who got jammed in the Multithermal Dry Heat Cabinet. His knob dropped off.'

'Blimey!'

'Luckily we found it under one of the duck boards, otherwise he might have done himself a nasty injury.'

'I'll be careful,' I say.

'Right. Well, I think that's it, then.' Doctor Tensor picks up his catapult and looks around for fresh prey.

'Are you sure you don't want to change your mind about those biscuits? They'll be three quid tomorrow.'

'No thank you!' I say.

'All right. Please yourself. Mind how you open the door. Don't let all the bluebottles out.'

'They wouldn't want to leave, would they?' I say. 'This must be the only place they can find any food.'

I close the door and start padding back towards my room. What a funny bloke! He must be making a bleeding fortune – and I bet he was giving that Winsome bird one when I knocked on the door. I wonder if she talks posh when she is on the job? If she is anything like some of those upper class birds I had when I was cleaning windows she probably effs and blinds with the best of them.

Normally, I would think a lot more about Miss Winsome but I am so sodding hungry that the packet of gingernuts is uppermost in my mind. I get back to my room and decide that sleep is the best answer. Once I can get my head down I will stop thinking about food.

I put on my pyjamas, munch half a tube of toothpaste and get into bed. Very comfortable it is – and very clean. I reckon they must have changed the sheets especially for me. I nearly slide out of bed twice. I try to close my eyes but the wind keeps me awake. I don't usually suffer from wind, but then I don't usually suffer from starvation either. Mum's cooking may be diabolical but at least it is filling. It is difficult to find space to put the bicarbonate of soda on the edge of my plate. Dear old Mum. I say some rotten things about her but she has never let me go to sleep hungry – racked with stomach-ache, yes, but not hungry.

'There we go. Little Suky-puky does poo poos and mumsy-wumsy opens a nice tin of din-dins.'

It is Mrs Chalfont talking to her repulsive little pooch. If she goes on rabbiting like that I can see Timmy-wimmy doing a puky-wuky.

My friend with the big knockers is clearly addressing her pet from the sun verandah next door and hardly has the little brute's shrill yelp disappeared towards the nearest tree than a delicious smell of nosh invades my hooter. Yes, it is incredible, isn't it? All of a sudden that tin of dog food smells like prime steak. I must be in a bad way. I try and bury my face in the pillow but it is no good. I cannot escape from the pong. A vision of gooey hunks of meat rich in Marylebone jelly dances before my eyes.

Why should that filthy little mut have it all? I have heard that many Chinese restaurants serve nothing else during a cat shortage. I try and struggle against my impulse but sheer naked greed gets the better of me. The sound of Mrs Chalfonts' french window closing has no sooner smote my lug holes than I am out of bed and making for the verandah. There it is, glistening in the moonlight and looking more tempting than Raquel Welch in my present state of hunger. I scramble over the balcony and drop to my knees beside the bowl marked 'Doggydins'. No sooner have I stretched out a mit than the four legged spider appears by my side.

'Grrrrrrrrrrrrh!!'

The growl, of course, is supplied by me and Suky backs away with her hair standing on end. I am a bad man to cross when it comes to sharing a bowl of dog food. The pooch looks as if it wants to argue the toss but a quick clip on the snout sends it scampering up to the other end of the verandah. I am sorry, dog lovers, but you must understand how hungry I am. It is not a very nice little dog, anyway. I realise that when it passes a motion of no confidence next to my balcony.

I am about to grab the booty and do a bunk back to my room when I happen to take a peep through the curtains into Mrs Chalfont's room. Well! I must say! I have seen a few things in my time – but really! Mrs Chalfont is lying on the bed wearing a frilly housecoat with blooming great roses all over it. Not very exciting, you say? Hang on a minute. I have not finished. It was not an electric toothbrush I heard on my way to supper. It was one of those electric vibrators that you use for soothing away aches and pains, releasing nervous tension and all that – Mrs Chalfont is using it for 'all that'.

It is a good job that I went to Copenhagen with the Fight Unclean Culture Korps otherwise I might be shocked. As it is, my 'Doggydins' bowl is trembling between my fingers. I can see why these Peeping Tom blokes are thinking of forming a union. Having a quiet shufti at someone when they don't know you are there is quite a turn on. I watch the elastic plastic go down for the third time and feel the cold air rush to greet my hampton as it lurches out to see what all the fuss is about. I am still hungry but I don't want to leave the entertainment that Mrs Chalfont is so thoughtfully providing. Settling into a more comfortable position I start to nosh from the bowl and keep watching through the chink in the curtain. It is not exactly a TV snack but it is as good as some of the stuff Mum dishes up. Unfortunately, the horrible little Yorkshire nastiness finds the sight of me putting away its dins more than it can stand and starts barking.

Mrs Chalfont has just braced her legs against the end of the bed and her housecoat has fallen open so you can imagine how I feel. Really choked! So help me, I could pound that hound.

'Shut up, you little basket!' I hiss.

But it doesn't do any good. Suky throws her head back

and starts yapping away fit to bust. Even when I chuck her some meat she doesn't stop. In desperation I snatch the little swine up and for a second a red mist swims before my eyes. If only there was a bit more meat on the tiny tyke . . .

'Suky! What's the matter – Oh! Mr Lea!'

'In the flesh,' I say, summoning up some of the verbal magnetism that has made me the toast of the Clapham Junction tea dance set.

'So I can see.' Mrs Chalfont wrenches her eyes from the gaping front of my pyjamas. 'May I ask what you are doing with Suky?'

I am so confused that I nearly tuck Suky away by mistake – it could have been very nasty. Surely Mrs Chalfont does not think that I –? No! It does not bear thinking about. I know we live in strange times but – 'Well?'

'I was just bringing her back,' I say. 'I left the french windows open for a breath of french – I mean, fresh air, and she came bounding in large as life. I think she wanted to sleep on the end of my bed but I knew you'd be worried so I brought her back. Who's a lovely girl, then? Who's Daddy's pride and joy? Who's just bitten Daddy's finger to the bone?'

I kid you not. The little bastard has just sunk its poisoned fangs into my flesh.

'Oh no! Naughty Suky! How could you do that to nice Mr. Lea?' Suky is quick to show her mistress how she did it and I release the treacherous pooch with a scream. Before I can start stamping, it streaks into the surrounding foliage.

'I've never known her do anything like that before,' says the horrified Mrs Chalfont.' Are you all right? You look quite pale.'

Probably because I have just had a decko at your cleavage, I think to myself. By the cringe! A man could suffocate down there. Mrs C. pulls her housecoat around her and takes me by the hand.

'I'd better put something on it,' she says.

'Uuuuhm,' I say. I allow myself to be led into the bedroom

and notice how Mrs C. casually pulls a coverlet over her vibrator.

'Sit down,' she says. 'We'll dunk it in something until the bleeding stops.'

'Sounds lovely,' I say.

'If you're not feeling too fragile we could hold it under the cold tap. It makes the veins contract and restricts the flow of the blood.'

'I prefer the dunking,' I say.

Mrs Chalfont looks at me searchingly and unwinds my fist. 'You're going to live,' she says.

'Is that a promise?'

Mrs Chalfont is not quite certain whether I am being fresh or referring to my lifespan. 'Hold this tissue,' she says. 'I've got some Dettol in one of my bags.'

I wince convincing as my fingers go into the cloudy liquid and admire the curve of Mrs Chalfont's knockers a few inches from my nose.

'How are you finding it here?' she asks.

I think of telling her that I *haven't* found it yet but decide that it is probably too early to expose her to my salty wit.

'Very nice,' I say. 'Everything is very clean. I could do with some more grub, though.'

'A little starvation won't do you any harm,' says Mrs C. 'I'm certain you can spare a few inches.'

For the right person, I think to myself. This bird doesn't half come out with some comical remarks. I wonder if she knows what she's saying?

'I feel so hungry,' I say.

'It'll pass. There are other hungers beside that for food.'

'Very true,' I say. I wonder if she is thinking what I am thinking. Probably, or she would not have made her last remark.

'I find that if I can take my mind off eating, it makes life much easier.' She takes my finger out of the glass and examines it. 'See how it's all wrinkled up?'

I close my legs and nod.

'That's why friends are so important here. The right relationship can make all the difference.' She lets her fingers run down to my wrist and starts stroking it. Something tells me that she has a message for me.

I lie back on the bed and close my eyes. It is a good move because when I open them, Mrs Chalfont is lying beside me.

'What big eyes you've got,' I say.

'All the better to see you with,' she says.

I look down at her bristols and raise an eyebrow. She laughs.

'Don't say it,' she says. 'I know they're big. That's what I'm here for.'

'It's a great reason,' I say. 'You could get a lot of people to stay here with those.'

'How's your finger?' she says.

Well, they say that flattery will get you anywhere, don't they?

'It's feeling a bit better,' I say, giving her a practical demonstration.

'I see what you mean,' she says, nibbling my ear. 'Ooooh! I like it when you do that.' Her hand strays down the front of my pyjamas and slides over percy like a gambler checking that there are fifty-two cards in the deck.

'Likewise,' I say politely. I must say that she has a point about one kind of hunger replacing an other. I have hardly thought about my stomach since I have been in the room – now Mrs Chalfont's stomach, that is a completely different story. I run my mits over her firm, round belly and feel her responding like a love-starved pussy – I mean the kind with four legs and a saucer of milk.

'Do you think my baby-one is all right?' she says.

'Fantastic,' I say. I would not have called it baby but –

'I was referring to Suky,' says my hostess. 'I don't want her to stay out too long. She's very sensitive, you know.'

'You told me,' I say, wondering whether to point out that I have my own pet, craving for entrance. Fortunately, Mrs

Chalfont has a firm grasp of my problem – possibly, too firm.

'I don't expect you feel very kindly disposed towards Suky?' she says.

'I've never had a lot of experience of animals,' I say. 'Mum used to have a goldfish, but I never got very attached to it. I tried teaching it tricks but unless you were an ant's egg it didn't have any time for you.'

'They're not very demonstrative,' says Mrs C. sympathetically. 'Does your mother still have it?'

'I think she's a bit past it,' I say. 'Still, you never know. There was this bloke when we went to the Isla de Amor. He—'

Mrs C. tries to bring her shudder under control. 'I meant, does your mother still have the goldfish?'

I shake my head. 'No. It was very sad. I was helping him make an attempt on the Over Water record when the telephone rang. It was my aunt Edna. She could talk the hind legs off a millipede – all four hundred thousand of them. When I got back to the sitting room, Cedric was cocooned in carpet fluff.'

'Your mother must have been very upset?'

'She took it very well, really. We put Cedric back in the tank and told her he had strangled himself to death while weaving a nest.'

Mrs Chalfont does not say anything for a few minutes and I imagine that she may be affected by my story. She obviously has a soft spot for animals – amongst other things. My digits aren't exactly probing the inside of a pencil sharpener.

'I think you have a fantastic body,' I say with feeling – lots of it.

'Let's get out of these silly things,' purrs Mrs Chalfont. She rises to her feet and crosses to the curtains to ensure that they are tightly shut. 'One has to be careful,' she says. 'There was a Peeping Tom making the rounds last time I was here.'

I share her shudder and watch the housecoat slide off her shoulders. She is wearing a black nylon nightie which crackles alluringly and percy trembles like a young sapling hearing the rumble of distant thunder.

Mrs C. comes over to the bed and starts undoing the buttons of my pyjama jacket. 'Off,' she says. 'I'm not giving you a free strip-tease, my body isn't up to it.'

'Let's have a look,' I say.

I slip out of my jacket and haul up her nightie like I am gathering in a net. Not a bad catch either. She presses forward and I disappear into her cleavage so that she would only have to slap the side of her titties to shut off my air supply. She is warmer than a plate of freshly buttered toast and I run my hands lightly over her curvaceous back bumpers – just playing a haunch, as they say.

She finishes taking off her nightie with a clumsy speed that suggests that her mood matches my own and I have to admire what I see. Generous might be the word to use when describing her ration of curves. She is stacked like the approach path to London airport and it is almost frightening to find yourself underneath those enormous knockers without a crash helmet on. Fortunately, I am in a mood to take risks.

I start to undo my pyjama cord but Mrs Chalfont brushes my fingers away. 'Allow me,' she says. 'You're a sick man. You don't want to take too much out of yourself.'

'That's what the vicar used to tell us,' I say. 'He was always on about it.'

Mrs Chalfont does not reply but rips down my pyjamas so fast that the cord burns the inside of my thigh.

'Careful!' I say. 'It's not much but it's all I've got.'

'It's beautiful,' asys Mrs C. 'You haven't seen my husband.'

'I definitely haven't!' I tell her. I don't want to hear about him either. Comparisons are odorous when it comes to the sack and I don't like to be reminded that I am on the point of shoving my love truncheon up some bloke's old lady's crutch hutch. I am very sensitive like that.

In order to cut short any more rabbit I apply my lips to the lady's cakehole and proceed to drown in their soft velvet texture. This bird is soft as a bunny's tummy and the more we kiss, the more I feel tingling currents popping off like miniature fire crackers. I pull her down onto the bed and she wriggles in a way that tells me that she wants me on top of her. Regular readers will know that I am not the kind of bloke to refuse a request like that and I leap to my knees. Like a greyhound straining at the slipperys – as Shakespeare might have put it – percy pants at the portal.

'Come on!' Mrs Chalfont yanks at my flanks and like a radar controlled missile my happy hampton romps into nookyville.

Have you ever been on one of those things at the fair that shakes you up and down? I don't know what they're called but the Bosky Dell version answers to the name of Chalfont, Mrs. What a performer! Maybe not in the first flower of youth but a very lovely growth all the same. Everything shudders like the Congolese State Ballet Company and I have to concentrate hard in order to contain my enthusiasm. The bed head is wacking against the wall and Suky is yapping on the verandah but Mrs Chalfont has her eyes tightly closed and is obviously a long way away from any local distractions.

'Now!' she yelps. 'Now! Now! Now!'

She speaks not a minute too soon. Despite thinking hard about concrete pencil cases and the future of comprehensive education I am unable to distract my mind from the outbreak of curves rioting beneath my body. Like a punctured balloon I seem to be racing round the room in ever diminishing size and circles until I come to rest with a wild squeak.

'That was gorgeous,' says Mrs C., hardly pausing to draw breath. 'Let's have a glass of Lucozade and do it again.'

It is four o'clock when I am eventually able to limp out

onto the verandah. Suky snaps at my ankle before racing inside but I am too knackered even to aim a kick at her. To make matters worse, the little bastard has finished up all the dog food.

## CHAPTER 5

In which Timmy becomes completely exhausted and receives the kiss of life in a sauna.

The next morning it is all I can do to get up – even with Mrs Chalfont helping me. Jesus, but she is a goer that woman! I must have left the French windows open because she and her blooming pooch came bounding up on the bed before I can get my eyes half open. Cold nose, wet tongue licking your face. It is a diabolical way to wake someone – and the dog isn't much better.

'I always think it's the nicest way to start the day,' says Mrs C., as she shoulders me to one side and scrambles under the sheets.

'Not in front of the dog!' I say. I mean, sitting there with its head to one side and its tongue hanging out, it makes me go all goose pimply. I would not mind so much if it would stop wagging its tail.

Eventually, I get rid of them both by pretending to have a heart attack. I don't have to act very hard either. I am so knackered I can hardly pull my trousers on. The combination of Mrs Chalfont and starvation is more shagging than skipping in a suit of armour.

I stagger into breakfast and my eye is greeted by what must be half a dwarf grapefruit, rocking from side to side at the bottom of a bowl. I mention 'sugar' and people stop eating five tables away. I never go a bundle on grapefruit at the best of times – not unless it comes out of a tin – and this one is so sour it makes the inside of my mouth pucker up like a tortoise's neck. Nevertheless, I am so hungry that I eat every bit of it and save the pips till last as a special treat. By the time I have had my rusk and a cup of herbal tea – unsweetened, of course – I have accumulated enough strength to crawl back to my room. It is just as well that I get out of the dining room when I do because the fresh green stalks of the flowers in the vase on my table are becoming almost irresistible.

'Hello, Weary Willy,' sings out Doctor Tensor, earning my respect for his instant diagnosis. 'Have a good breakfast?'

'Smashing,' I say. 'You don't need a cook in this place, do you? Just a bloke to open the packets of biscuits.'

'Don't be like that, my old mate,' says Dr T. scraping the egg off his Old Etonian tie – I know it is an Old Etonian tie because it has 'Old Etonian' embroidered all over it. 'You need a bit of rhythmical exercise. Put your track suit on and bugger off to the gym.'

'What's that?' I asked.

'It's a large room with wall bars and ropes and all that caper.'

'I know that!' I hiss the words through clenched teeth. 'I meant, what is rhythmical exercise?'

'Doing exercises to music. I always recommend that because I know what it is. I know what a colonic lavage is but I don't recommend that.'

'Thanks,' I say.

'It's difficult to keep track,' says Tensor. 'I wish you'd have Short Wave Diathermy then you could tell me what it is.'

'Why don't you have it yourself?' I ask.

Dr T. shakes his head firmly. 'How do you think I found out what a colonic lavage was?'

I find that a little conversation with Doctor Tensor goes a long way and having failed to negotiate the sale of a packet of tea-time assorted for three pounds fifty I stumble back to my room to change.

Starvation is having an effect on me already because my rib cage looks like it should have a bleeding vulture sitting in the middle of it. When I put on a pair of shorts I have to tie a knot in the elastic to keep them up. I do hope the rhythmical exercises take my mind off food.

They don't, of course. All the songs we wave our arms about to are connected with nosh. 'You're the Cream in my Coffee', 'A Spoonful of Sugar' – it makes you sick, it really does. When the stupid old bag who takes us puts on 'Food, Glorious Food' I nearly burst into tears.

Despite my suffering I can't help noticing that there are some quite sprauncy birds about. Not exactly in the first flush of youth but in much better nick than the blokes. They are really diabolical, some of them. Talk about 'I haven't seen my little Willy'. Their bellys are practically spilling into their socks. Just to look at them makes me feel like Charles Atlas. It is ridiculous me starving myself because if I ate like a pig for the whole two weeks I would still be in better shape than them if they never touched another thing. That is what makes it so unfair. They have their fat to live off. My stream-lined hulk has not got a built-in larder.

The birds are all wearing leotards – black body stockings to you, mate. You have probably seen ballet dancers using those mirrors with rails to test them for holes. It is one of the ways they have of supplementing their meagre earnings. Anyway, they are quite a turn on if you fancy black stockings and I most certainly do. I have only got to see a nurse and I get a lump in my trousers. I notice that the bints are much more agile than the blokes and do not puff and wheeze like Ted Heath playing his organ with a leak in it. They are also not above flashing the glad eye and I reckon that Mrs Chalfont must have quite a few kindred spirits on board. That lady gives me a wink as she pushes out her pelvis and I make plans to wedge something under my door knob. Normally I would count myself well-favoured by the presence of such a lanky curve-carnival in the next door room but in my present condition she is less use to me than a calorie counter. Where does she get the energy from? You only have to look at the blokes to realise that they are knackered to a man while the birds are throbbing with high spirits and vitality. It is as if they thrive on starvation while the blokes peg out.

When the session is over I hardly have the strength to drag

myself back to my room. I collapse on the bed and gonk until it is time for what they call 'luncheon' at Bosky Dell. I have heard this described as the big meal of the day and it is in a state bordering on that of uncontrollable excitement that I launch myself through the door of the dining room. Summoning up my last resources of energy I stagger to the table unaided and flop down in front of a plate containing three radishes. On the table next to me, the bird has four radishes and only lack of strength prevents me from throwing myself at her throat.

She has obviously been having it away with one of the waiters. A glance at them shows that they obviously get all the radishes they need – ruddy complexions, bulging limbs. It makes you sick.

'Are you partial to radishes?'

It is the bird at the next table and she is holding out her plate.

'Well I – er, yes, thank you very much.' I snatch the radishes and shove a few into my mouth in case someone tries to take them away from me.

'It's cod today,' says the bird. 'The piece of cod that passeth man's understanding.'

I nod brightly and wonder what she is talking about. My God, but these radishes taste good. It is marvellous to know that your gnashers can still function.

I sit back and deliver a loud burp. I suppose if you gobble radishes you are asking for trouble. 'Pardon,' I say.

'My name is Jane Arkright,' says the bird. 'Is this your first time here?'

'Timothy Lea,' I say. 'First and last. I can't exist on the grub they give you here.'

Mrs Arkright – I presume she is a Mrs – is a nice looking article with curly blonde hair that makes her look younger than she probably is. It also makes her look as if she wants to look younger than she really is. Birds like that are often eager for any opportunity to show that the sap is still rising. Unfortunately my sap has sunk so low that if I was wearing open-toed sandals there would be puddles on the carpet.

'Yes. The portions are meagre,' says Mrs Arkwright. 'Quite out of keeping with all the appurtenances.'

'Exactly,' I say. 'And I can't see why they need all the knives and forks.'

'I think it gives everyone the impression that they're getting their money's worth,' says Mrs A. 'If you sat down at a scrubbed wood table and were handed a carrot you might resent paying a hundred pounds for the privilege. When it is presented to you on a silver salver and the wall is hung with de Hoochs you are more prepared to accept that the fees are justified.'

'I wouldn't mind a spotta de hooch,' I say. 'I don't reckon that nuns' water overmuch.'

'Monks' water,' corrects Mrs Arkwright. 'Yes, it does leave something to be desired.' Her nostrils flare. 'It's not the lack of food that disturbs me about this place, it's the lack of service.' She leans towards me confidentially. 'I can't get anyone to look at my plug-hole.'

'You amaze me,' I say.

Mrs Arkwright nods her head slowly. 'It's a fact. I mentioned it to Dr Tensor and – well, I won't tell you what he said.' She looks round before continuing. 'You know, there's something about that man I don't warm to. People say he's very good but I find him rather coarse.'

'I can understand that,' I say, swallowing a burp and wondering if the person sitting at the table on my right is going to want her radishes. If I nick them she won't have the problem of making up her mind, will she?

'I wonder if you would mind having a look at it? I'm certain it's the kind of thing a man could fix in a jiffy.'

My hand is snaking out towards the radishes, assisted in its purpose by an upwards movement of my fife, when a thought assails me. Is Mrs Arkwright only interested in her plug-hole or does she have an interior motive? I remember a little number at Melody Bay Holiday Camp who asked me round to look at her bedside lamp and spent most of her time showing me something quite different. I did not write to Fred Pontin about it but in those days I was on three meals a day and had enough strength to get my giggle stick into the vertical. At the moment I would be pushed to clamber into a tart's grumble if it was my birthday and you gave me a set of splints.

'I'm afraid I'd just make a mess of it,' I say. 'I'm hopeless with things like that.'

Mrs Arkwright sniffs and looks as if she would like to ask for her radishes back. Oh, the shame of it! South London's champion hampton parker backing off like a neutered natter-jack. I am so choked that when my cod arrives I eat it without noticing it. Only the small skid mark in the middle of the plate tells me it was there. I still feel as empty as Brixton Town Hall during an 'I Love Enoch Powell' rally. This is it! I can't take any more – or rather, I can't take any less. If I don't get some nosh I'll be brown bread.

Nodding politely to Mrs Arkwright, who ignores me, I head back to my room and pocket some mazuma. There must be a village nearby that has some shops. I will nip out and do my Cousin Kelly a favour.

I get outside the front door and there is Baines squeezing out his chamois. He gives me an old-fashioned look and then gets on with cleaning the Rolls. I think about asking for a lift but he does not look the giving type.

The drive seems a mile long when you are knocking it off on your plates and my kangas are really giving me gip by the time I get to the wrought iron gates. I am not over-chuffed to find that they are padlocked. I am contemplating picking a path through the privet when a crunch like a spoon going into a bowl of sugar alerts me to the fact that the Rolls has crept up behind me. Baines rests his arm on the window and flashes his Edwards at me. It is not the most sincere smile I have ever received.

'Going somewhere?' he says.

'Trying to,' I say. 'How do you get out of this place except in a slim coffin?'

'You get a pass out from Doctor Tensor.'

I control myself with difficulty. 'Don't talk to me about "pass outs"!' I snort. 'I bleeding nearly passed out on the way down here. If I don't get some food inside me I'm a gonner.'

Baines jerks his finger up the drive. 'You can't break your diet without Doctor Tensor gives the OK. It's in the rules.' Quite where we would go from there I don't know because, at that moment, two middle-aged geezers wearing track suits run out of the bushes.

'It's mine! It's mine!' squeaks the first one. 'I caught it!'

'It was my idea!' says the second one. 'You'd said we'd share—' He breaks off when he sees us.

The first bloke is holding something pink and wriggling at crotch level – yes, I thought that, too, but it turns out to be a goldfish.

'Put that back, this instant!' bellows Baines. 'You know you're not allowed to fish in the ornamental lake – and you! Yes, you! You've been digging up bulbs again, haven't you?'

The other bloke tries to put his dirty germans behind his back but Baines leaps out of the jam jar and tugs the front of his track suit. Half a dozen bulbs, three onions and a stick of celery fall out.

'Going to have a banquet, were you?' says Baines.

'Have a heart,' says the bloke. 'We're starving.'

'That's not my problem,' says Baines. 'I'm here to protect the property. I can't afford to jeopardise my position and the high standards which pertain in this institution by countenancing any irregularity.'

'We'll make it worth your while,' says the bloke with the Lilian Gish.

'How much?' says Baines.

A few minutes later the transaction has been completed and Baines is tucking a Lady Godiva into his sky. Now it is my turn to corrupt the bugger.

'How much to let me out?' I say.

'Not a chance.' Baines shakes his head. 'There's too much of it going on.'

If I had the strength, and he was a bit smaller, I would do him. The Charley 'Arstard does not even offer me a lift up the drive.

When I get back to the Mickey Mouse everybody is still recovering from Jim Skinner and I can't help clocking that a lot of female minces are giving me the once over.

'You don't play bridge, do you?' says an aristocratic bint and three pairs of pleading eyes look up at me from a green beige Aesop.

'I've never had the pleasure,' I say civilly. 'Strip poker is more my Charles Forte.'

I mean it as a little joke but the birds look quite interested. Harm could come to a young boy – if he was lucky enough not to be knackered. I head towards my room but I have only taken half a dozen steps down the corridor when a door opens and Mrs Arkwright pops out.

'Oh,' she says, all surprised like. 'It's you.'

'Now you come to mention it, so it is,' I say. 'Don't let me disturb you. I must—'

'Have a look at my plumbing,' she says. 'Please!' For some reason best known to herself, she has unbuttoned her blouse and is revealing a half cup bra filled to the brim with luscious threepenny bits. In my normal condition I would be round her S bend before you could say 'Roger Carpenter with knobs on', but now it is just not there. I would find it easier to get up the Post Office Tower in a wheelchair.

'I'm sorry,' I say. 'I'm feeling a bit uncle. I think it must be those radishes. I hope you get yourself sorted out.'

I do too, but I don't envy the next bloke who has her. You know what they say: beware the furry of a woman scorned.

I take off down the corridor and if she is singing 'For He's a Jolly Good Fellow' I don't hear it. The sooner I am tucked away in my David Broome, the better.

I stretch out my hand for the knob – thank you, madam. I thought of that, too – and then pause. Suky's shrill yap rings in my bottles. Have I come to the wrong room by mistake? I drop to my knees and take a quick butchers through the keyhole. No, those are my pants. I would recognise that shade of beige anywhere. But it is not my fleas and ants that grab my attention – it is what is lying on my Uncle Ned: Mrs Chalfont in the altogether. She is not pressing my best whistle, that is for sure.

So much for my afternoon nap. I can forget that. Once through the door I will be rising and falling on Mrs C., knockers like a loose bra. Bless you, Suky. Maybe I won't poison you after all. But what am I going to do? Where can I go to get my head down – and I am not talking about a muff job.

I tiptoe away from my room and decide to indulge in a spot of Egyptian P.T. in one of the public lounges. In a place this size there must be somewhere where the residents can snuff it in peace. I come round the corner and – sod it! There is Mrs Arkright. I don't want to bump in to her. There is a door marked 'SAUNA' on my right and I push through it sharpish. I am in a small changing room with another door leading off it marked 'Sauna – insure that this door is closed at all times'.

I take a look beyond the second door and it is like trying to cook your loaf with the Christmas turkey. Talk about hot! I can hardly breathe – watch it! I heard that. The room has wooden benches going up in steps one behind the other and a charcoal brazier. You could get the Ted Heath fan club in there, no trouble – mind you, Ted might feel a bit lonely but I expect that he gets used to that.

There is no one about and it occurs to me that this is probably as good a place to kip as any – I might even do myself a bit of good. I'm going to lose weight, that's for certain. You could not do anything else in this heat. I strip off my these and those and pad into the sauna. There is no one else about so I climb up to the top bench and stretch out on the wooden slats. I seem to remember something about rolling in the snow and being beaten with birch twigs, but they can stuff that for a lark. Timothy will stay here until it is time for his grilled lettuce leaf, and forget the hearty stuff.

A trickle of sweat runs down my Ned Kelly and my eyes begin to sting. By the cringe but it is hot – so hot that it hurts to breathe. I hope they know what they're doing. I'd hate a giant hand to come in and turn me over for another five minutes like some blooming tea cake. I close my minces and when I open them I am not alone. A naked human being is in the act of closing the door. Starkers, but holding a towel in her hand. Yes *her*. It is a bird – unless the heat plays disappearing tricks with your nuts. On close inspection, the lady is not unknown to me. It is Miss Winsome.

She recognises me about the time I get a definite fix on her.

'Ee-oh,' she says. 'You're a man.'

'Flattery will get you anywhere, darling,' I say. 'Do you come here often?'

'This is the women's period,' she says, tapping a piece of paper on the wall. For a moment I think I have blundered into a lecture on the menstrual cycle and then I see what she is getting at.

'Is it really?' I say. 'Oh I am sorry. I didn't notice.' I glance at my watch and find that all the hands are sliding about behind the glass. They must have been steamed out of their moorings.

'The tea-imes are in the brochure. There's a key-opy in reception if you've mislaid the wee-un in your room.'

This chick obviously imagines that I have time to read brochures when I am in my bedroom. She does not know the half or it.

'Do you want me to go?' I say. I notice that she has not bothered to wrap her towel round herself so she can't be too horrified by what she is clocking.

'No.' Miss Winsome shakes her head slowly. 'It dee-oesn't matter. We'd bee-etter protect those of a more nee-ervous dee-isposition, though.' She slinks over and does something to the door. She has a very trim little body and a lovely set of back bumpers. In another world I would like to give her a game of Dodgems and handle any damage on a knock for knock basis. When her back is turned I separate percy from my inside leg measurement and run the sweat off my eyebrows – not with my Mad Mick, of course, I do have a bit of decorum.

'Are you – er locking it?' I ask nervously.

'We dee-ont wee-ont to free-ighten anybody, do we?'

Her body is glistening seductively in the gloom and she removes a beckoning finger of hair that has become stuck to her cheek and comes towards me. Oh my gawd! I always reckoned it was like this in the Turkish baths. Either that or Bernard Dillons locking you in the steam cabinets. I draw my knees up so that I could rest my chin on them and await developments.

'How did you knee-ow I was going to be here?' The saucy minx sits down in front of me and rests her back against my scotches.

'I didn't know,' I say. 'I just happened to fancy a – a sauna. You know how it is?'

Miss Winsome turns to look up at me and I snap my knees together like nut crackers.

'Pull the other one, mate!' she says.

'I beg your pardon?'

'Don't give me that pony and trap. I could see you were after a Friar Tuck the minute you took a gander at me.'

What has happened to that nicely spoken lady behind the reception desk? Can my bottles be deceiving me?

'You don't normally speak like that.'

'Oh yes I bleeding do. Don't let the posh rabbit two foot rule you. I bubble and squeak just like my old man.'

'Doctor Tensor,' I breathe. Zo, Heinrich. She iz ze daughter ov ze commandant. Interestink, nein? Oh vel, pleaze yourzelv.

'Yeah. Don't you notice the resemblance?'

I look down at the moist and inviting Sheila before me and do a quick comparison with the bald-headed old piss artist who swopped a few dicky birds with me behind the sign of Doctor Tensor.

'In a word: not on your nelly,' I say. 'Why do you bother to put on all that posh bit?'

'It was my dad's idea. He said that you can only have one rough diamond amongst a load of cultured pearls.'

'How beautifully expressed,' I gasp. I gasp for two reasons. One, because my vocal chords have been charred. Two, because Miss Tensor's eel-like arm is gliding up my leg like it knows where it is going.

'What hairy scotches you've got,' she says, like the idea appeals to her.

'Hang on a minute,' I say. 'I think there's something you ought to know.'

'We know all about you,' she says, cheerfully.

Her words strike cold terror into my heart – and believe me, that is some achievement in this heat. They must have realised that I stuck out like a spare prick at a whore's wedding and done some checking up.

'There's no harm in looking,' I say.

'Looking?' says the bird. 'You're a male nail, aren't you?'

'A what?' I say.

'A brass nail, a tail, a gigolo. You're not the first we've had here. Earning a bit of pocket money for doing what comes naturally.'

'You must be joking!' I tell her. 'I'm knackered. I couldn't give Raquel Welch one for the price of a love dive.'

'Saving yourself for the paying customers, eh?' says the bird, standing up. 'Do you really prefer their bodies to mine?' She grabs one of my mits – eventually. It slips out of her grasp twice – and puts it on one of her Manchesters.

'I don't want to give offence,' I say. 'But I'm not in the mood. The heat, the lack of food. I've hardly got the strength to pull my socks up.'

'But it's fantastic in here!' says Doctor Tensor's little girl eagerly. 'Feel my body. Slippery, glistening—'

She is doing all the talking but she is also doing all the

feeling. I must be in a bad way because percy is playing up like a dead battery. There is not a twitch or a tremor out of him. I can hardly feel her fingers through him.

'You're not bent, are you?' says Miss T.

'Bent!!?? I'm not bent, I'm starving to death!' What do you have to do to get through to this bird.

'It must be the heat,' she says. 'You need a cold plunge.'

I am not so certain that she is right but before I can think about it she has grabbed my Chalk Farm.

'I think I'll nip back to my room for a lie down,' I say.

'This way.' She pulls open a door and I start scrambling up some steps before I know what I am doing. Suddenly, before me, is a small, deep pool. I can tell by looking at it that it is very, very cold.

'I think I'd better—' You can fill in the scream and the splash for yourselves.

Miss Tensor has reached between my legs and given my rip cord a tug. Charming, isn't it? I can see her passing round the crumpets at the vicar's tea party.

I don't say anything because I can't say anything. Not a dicky bird. I can hear myself making a gasping noise but nothing gets further than the back of my throat. Talk about taters! If I was a brass monkey I would need a welding job. I struggle to the side of the bath just as Miss Tensor leaps in.

'Bleeding invigorating, isn't it?' she says.

If she is referring to the way her knockers bound about when she plays roundabouts I would have to agree with her but I think she is talking about the water temperature.

'Don't you feel better?' she says.

'I don't feel anything,' I say. I haul myself out the bath and – blimey! I don't see anything, either. Mr Whoopee has abbreviated himself to Mr Wee. I've seen acorns with more charisma. What is more, there is an unhealthy blue tint which is definitely not this season's colour.

'Look what you've done!' I yelp.

'Where?' she says.

'That's just it!' I scream. 'You can't see it any more!'

'Don't worry,' she says briskly with her bristols bristling. 'It's adjusting itself to your body temperature. It's like the mercury in a barometer. When it gets cold it sinks into the bottom.'

'I don't want it to sink into my bottom!' Blimey! She knows how to paint a pretty picture this bird.

'Don't be a berk,' she says, charmingly. 'I wasn't referring to your Elephant and Castle.'

'There's no sensation,' I whimper.

'I don't want to be unkind, ducky. But it wasn't causing a heck of a lot of sensation to start off with.'

'You don't seem to understand,' I say, my voice quavering. 'I have got frost bite of the hampton and you're treating it as if it is nothing.'

'I didn't say it was nothing,' says the cruel bitch. 'I just suggested that I wouldn't put it forward for the Guinness Book Of Records.'

'That reminds me,' I say. 'I read about a bloke who had the same problem and he dipped his wick in brandy.'

'You've had that,' says Miss Tensor helpfully. 'The only brandy in the place belongs to my old man and he likes to warm it up with his hands.'

'It's me who needs the warming,' I yelp.

'Get back in the sauna,' she says. 'That's all it needs. You've never had a heart attack, have you?'

'No. Why?'

'It doesn't matter. I should have asked you before you went in the cold bath.'

Marvellous, isn't it? If I get out of this place with all my pieces in a cardboard box I will be lucky. The heavy door swings open and the now delicious warmth presses against me like hot towels.

'Isn't there something we can dip it in?' I say, pathetically. When I say 'dip' I am boasting. My old man is like a cigar butt sitting on a couple of walnuts. I could not dip it in a saucer of milk and guarantee to hit bottom.

'Lie down,' says Miss Tensor.

'Why?' I say.

'I'm going to help you,' says Miss T. calmly. 'I'm going to soothe you, calm you, ease your fears and bring you pleasure all in one delicious experience.'

'Where do you want me to lie?' I say. I mean you don't start arguing the toss when you get an offer like that, do you? What have I got to lose that may not have gone already?

'On the top boards.'

I do as I am told and Miss T. drapes herself on the step below me. Her mouth is half open and she leans over me so that her wet hair brushes against my shoulders.

'Ready?' she says.

'Uuuhm.'

She kisses me gently on the lips and her fingers fiddle with the foliage round my filbert before tip-toeing down my body to tweak at the thatch round my tonk. Down in the forest something stirs. It may not be springtime in Hampton Park but at least there is a crack in the ice age.

'Relax.' Why do birds say things like that when they are making you go rigid? Her mouth follows the path made by her fingers and her tongue glides along like a soft shock machine. My shoulder blades are not touching the boards by the time she collides with my disaster area.

'Tell me when you feel something,' she says.

Talk about a golden retriever! This judy can fetch my balls any day of the week. In no time at all the magic kiss of life is working wonders with the afflicted quarter. Numbness turns into feeling, turns into sensation, turns into sensational! Her fingers tweak, stroke and massage and percy begins to return to his normal state – the orange free state. Great O.Kays out of little acorns grow.

'Am I getting through to you?' husks my friend.

'I think you're through the other side,' I gasp. 'Tell me,

have you ever thought of taking up the trumpet?'

'I had a session with a French horn, once,' says the bird. She raises her head and sweeps her barnet to one side. 'There we are. I think you'll be able to plant spuds with that.'

I look down and there is percy rearing up towards me. It is an affecting moment as you can imagine and somewhere, in the back of my mind, I hear the theme tune from Dr Zhivago. If you feel like shedding a quiet tear, don't mind me.

'That's wonderful,' I sob. 'Whatever can I do to thank you?'

Half an hour later I am back in my room. I don't know how I got there but I suspect that someone poured me through the keyhole. Miss Tensor said something about dropping in on me after supper and I reckon that is all I need. Making love in that sauna took more out of me than I had in the first place. I have lost so much weight that when I stood sideways in front of the mirror I got lost against the striped wallpaper. Thank God Mrs Chalfont had pushed off when I got back. If she had got her mits on me I would have been a gonner. As it is I hardly dare breathe in case she or her perishing pooch hear me. What a carve up. And to think that this place calls itself a temple of physical fitness. I have never been in a worse state in my life. I have got to get out, there is no doubt about it. Just at that moment there is a tap on the door and I nearly jump out of my skin – not an easy thing to do in my present condition. If I lie still perhaps they will go away.

'Mr Lea? It's me, Cedric.'

A man at least, though the high-pitched voice doesn't sound like Kenneth McKeller.

'What do you want?' I whisper.

'I want to have a few words with you.'

Blast the bleeder! For two pins I would tell him to piss off except that I don't want to alert Mrs C.. I lift the armchair off the table and pull it away from the door. The bloke standing outside has yellow hair and is wearing blue eye shadow. It is definitely not Kenneth McKeller.

'Can I come inside?' He says.

'You already have,' I say, turning round. He moves fast, this bloke.

'I brought it for you,' he says, shoving a paper into my germans.

*Gay News.* I reach behind me for a towel and wish that the family owned a dressing gown. I must ask Mum to knit me one for Christmas. That scarf of hers is getting nowhere.

'I don't quite understand,' I say, trying to show him that I don't need any help to wrap a towel round me.

'Roll it up and tuck it down the front,' he says. 'Here. Let me.'

'I can do it, thank you!' I say. 'Look. I don't read *Gay News.* There must be a mistakes.'

Cedric looks disappointed. 'Mrs Arkwright said you were bemoaning its absence from the reading room.'

'That was *Penthouse,*' I say, understanding all. How typical of the spiteful nature of some women. As if I did not have enough problems on my hands.

'She said you didn't like it here. I don't like it here either.' Cedric sits down on my bed and crossing one leg over the other clasps his hands round a knee. 'I haven't found a single kindred spirit.'

'Tough,' I say.

'I thought it was going to be lovely when I came – and of course it is lovely when you come—'

'I know what you mean,' I say hurriedly.

Cedric starts rocking backwards and forwards. 'But apart from the gardens which are delightful, I have to admit that, it's been no fun at all. I haven't met anyone. Terrible businessmen, terrible women. No reciprocity.'

'It was nice of you to look in,' I say, advancing firmly towards the door. 'I'm sorry I'm not—'

'I came here because I was run down. Advertising. You have to be on your toes the whole time. Can't afford to slip behind.' Cedric shows no sign of taking the hint. 'Clients, executives. Everybody on at you. No respect for artistic integrity. They grind you down. I've tasted the bottom in the last few weeks, I don't mind telling you.'

'I can imagine,' I say, my hand on the doorknob.

Cedric looks round the room. 'Nice place you've got here. Big. Big bed, too. Two people could share very easily. It wouldn't be so lonely, would it?'

'Don't forget your magazine.'

'Your towel's slipping.'

'I can manage!'

'Let me give you a hand.'

'No.'

'Come on.'

'No!'

'I'm only trying to help.'

'Get off me!!'

Blimey! You have to give him full marks for trying. I have no sooner got the door open than he is all over me. My towel hits the deck and a battery of bints passing down the corridor catch the full lustre of my cluster. What must they think!? *Gay News* fluttering to the floor and Timothy tangling with Cedric in the altogether. Sounds like the autumn cover of *Butch Male.*

I slam the door on my embarrassment and examine my plight. Luckily, it appears to be unharmed. I have hardly got my breath back than there is a yap at the door.

'Timothy, I want to talk to you.' It is Mrs Chalfont.

That's it! I'm off. Anywhere. Instant scarper. I look out of the French windows and hope to see a helicopter left over from a bath salts advertisement. If I don't get out of Bosky Dell fast I'm going to end up fertilising the turnips. Next time, Sid can do his own dirty work.

'Come on, Timmy. Don't be a silly boy. I know you're in there.'

Not for long, Mrs Chalfont! I have got to do a bunk. But where? Suddenly, dead opposite the terrace, there is a dust cart. A bloke chucks a load of goods in the back and in a blinding flash of inspiration and fish heads I see my means of escape. As the vehicle taxis out of sight, I wrap my towel round me and shove everything I can lay my hands on into my bag. It is a shame I have to move so fast because there are a few coat hangars, ash trays and assorted objets d'art I would have liked to have packed for Mum. She has always had a leaning towards a touch of the gracious living and a coat hanger with 'Bosky Dell' on it would have gone down a treat. We might even have put it on the front door.

With my gear streaming in the wind I shoot through the French windows and leave the sound of Mrs Chalfont and dog behind. The dust cart is just turning into the drive and for a man in my condition the effort required to catch it up can only be described as superhuman. Each step is agony, but somehow I manage to chuck my gear in the back and prepare to scramble after it.

Oh dear! I had not realised that it was one of those dust carts that chews everything up. While I watch helplessly two steel arms claw my bag and set of steel jaws and it disappears from view.

I don't have a lot of time to think about it because the dust cart starts to move down the drive. I leap on the back and try to keep out of the way of the crusher as it churns round in front of me. As we go through the front gates my towel falls off.

# CHAPTER 6

In which Timmy goes home to Mum and Dad and later learns the Kung Fu massage technique from Miss Nishi and her Japanese helpmates.

'That's nice, isn't it?' says Dad. 'Stark bollock naked on the doorstep. I bet the neighbours liked that.'

'I wasn't naked,' I say, patiently. I was wearing a dustbin bag.'

'Yes, Dad. Fair's fair,' says Sid, all sarcastical. 'You mustn't exaggerate. There's a lot of difference between wandering around in your birthday suit and wearing a nice, shiny black bag. It's quite sartorial by today's standards.'

'No need for that kind of language, foul mouth,' says Dad, spitting all over his suet pudding. 'I don't know where he gets it from, I really don't. Give him half a chance and he's prancing around in the buff. It's not natural. Nobody else in the family does it.'

'That's not strictly true,' says Mum. 'I remember your mother going on about your Aunty Madge. Used to terrorise them on Wandsworth Common, she did. She'd run out of the bushes with her skirt held up saying "I am a lapwing defending my young. Follow me and save my chicks." '

'Ridiculous!' says Dad.

'Oh no it's not!' says Mum, firmly. 'I remember at our wedding there was some unpleasantness. I was in the vestibule at the time.'

'You were in the karsi, most of the time,' says Dad.

'If I'd known what I was letting myself in for, I'd have stayed there,' says Mum. 'Anyway, don't change the subject. Your Aunty Madge got up to her tricks and the vicar asked her to leave. Mind you, I don't know what he thought *he* was doing. You remember that nice young Penny Carter? Well, she said—'

'All right, all right!' says Dad. 'You don't have to go on. So there is a president for his unplesant behaviour.'

'You mean "precedent",' I say.

'No, he's referring to President Nixon,' says Sid.

'What are you on about?' says Dad.

'It was a political joke,' says Sid. 'A bit above your head – like what I would like the waters of the Thames to be. You still reckon George Washington is on the throne across there, don't you?'

'Oh. Talking about the Ham Shanks, are you?' says Dad. 'That's where all your trouble comes from. Your decadence and your Mecca dance—'

'And your streaking!' says Sid. 'That's what he's been doing all these years. He was at it long before the Yanks got hold of the idea.'

'Don't take the piss. I had a bit of bad luck, that's all.'

'Very true,' says Sid. 'You have to sympathise with any bloke who chucks all his clothes in a garbage nosher, don't you? Every Friday I have to restrain myself when the dust cart comes round. It's the same all down the street. Old age pensioners ripping off their drawers and flinging them in the back with shouts of maniacal glee. I've seen Mum quivering a bit.'

'Shut your cake-hole, you dirty 'Arstard! You're no bleeding Jeremy Thorpe when it comes to conducting yourself in public.'

'That's right, Dad,' I say. 'You tell him. He's got a cruel tongue.'

Any hopes I have of wrestling a little sympathy from my disgusting parent are doomed to disappear up the spout.

'Belt up, Lady Godiva!' he shouts. 'You go on shovelling nosh into your cakehole! Food that I've sweated and slaved to provide. While you and that sponging, no good brother in law of yours ponce about trying to get something for nothing, decent working class blokes like me—' Dad breaks off to waggle his finger under Sid's nose. '—and I'm not ashamed to say I'm working class!'

'I know you're not,' says Sid. 'You expect to get a bleeding medal for it!'

'There's medals been given for worse,' says Dad, tellingly. 'Medals *and* honours.'

'Aaaargh! That be right, Jim Lad.' Sid rolls his eyes.

'You can't take nothing serious, can you?' yells Dad. 'Bleeding country going to the dogs and you're not prepared to do anything about it. It's people like you what are the reason why we are where we are today.'

'You've lost me now, Dad.'

'I wish I bleeding could!!' shouts Dad. 'Lose the both of you. Lazy load of gits. Look at him with custard all round his cakehole.' He is pointing his finger at me. 'He's like a bleeding pig! It's disgusting!'

'It is too,' says Sid. 'That's supposed to be a Yorkshire pudding he's noshing. You've got to cook it, Mum!'

'Don't tell your mother-in-law how to cook,' snaps Dad. 'What she doesn't know about cooking is worth knowing.'

'You can say that again!' says Sid.

'He's not complaining, is he?' says Dad. 'You don't hear him whining and wingeing.'

'That's because he's had his cakehole jammed full from the moment he came through the door. Brrrh, brrrh! – Over the gas masks – Crackle, crackle – half a loaf of bread in his gob before you can say "How's your father?" '

It is a fact. I never thought the day would come when I attacked Mum's cooking – well, you know what I mean – but hunger does strange things to you. Raw Yorkshire pudding can taste very nice when you're starving.

'It's good to see the boy eating again,' says Mum. 'I was worrying about him losing his appetite.'

'Yeah.' Sid looks at Mum thoughtfully. 'In the long run he'd probably lose more weight here than he would at a health clinic. I should have thought of that when I was planning the catering for Beauty Manor. You could have been our cook, Mum. How do you fancy the idea of being a domestic bursar?'

'Don't answer him!' says Dad. 'I know who's the biggest bursar round here, mate!'

'How is Beauty Manor?' I ask hurriedly, looking round for something to wipe my north and south on. Mum offers her apron but I don't fancy that. It looks like something you lay the bits on when you're doing an oil change. I use the back of my hand and scrape it on the underside of the table. There is a ledge there containing bits of Mum's cooking I have been accumulating since I was a kiddy.

'Marvellous,' says Sid. 'We're opening in a couple of days. Everything is looking great and we're booked out on the strength of the brochure and what Sir Henry has been telling his mates.'

'I'm looking forward to my trip ever so much,' says Mum. 'I reckon I'm going to feel a new woman. What about you, Dad?'

'I reckon he'd feel a new woman if you gave him half a chance!' says Sid.

This remark is not well received by either my mother or my father and the rest of my conversation with Sid is conducted in the public bar of the Hand and Racket. I give him a run down on what I have seen at Bosky Dell and he nods his head wisely.

'Yeah. I think we've taken care of everything. The basic principle is that as long as you stand still and don't touch anything, it's free – apart from the initial hundred quid for tea and cabbage leaves. But that's like going into an amusement arcade and not playing any of the tables. Nobody can do that. We've lined up a load of lovely goodies they won't be able to resist: Electrophyschotic Faradism, Underwater Hynosis, Neuro Muscular Dietetics, Hydrotherapeutic Ultrasonics—'

'Blimey, Sid. That must have cost a fortune.'

'It did. But as Wanda says: "in for a penny, infra red." Get it?' My wince tells him that I do. 'Once they get involved in the extras then the prices escalate. We're reckoning on doubling the basic hundred quid fee – and that's just by treatments.'

'What else is there?'

'There's the restaurant and off-sales.'

'Who's going to eat at the restaurant?'

'Two lots of people: Guests who can't stand the starvation and their visitors or people who just want to wander in and use the amenities.'

'You mean, the lavs?'

'No, you berk! The swimming pool, the bar, the restaurant.'

'You're having a bar? You weren't allowed to touch the stuff at Bosky Dell.'

'It doesn't make sense to me,' says Sid. 'I like the idea of a bar for two reasons. One. Because of the profit. Two. Because if you didn't get any benefit from your visit and you'd had a few tumbles you'd only have yourself to blame. We want people to come back and say: 'I'll steer clear of the temptations this time and really do myself a bit of Robin Hood' – and again, and again . . .'

'It sounds appropriately diabolical to me, Sid. Did you think all this up?'

'Some of it,' says Sid. 'I find it very useful having Wanda to fall back on.'

'I can imagine.'

'Yes. She has a lot of experience of this kind of thing and a very shrewd business brain. It's amazing what she can wheedle out of people. Sir Henry is like putty in her hands.'

'And is Rosie looking after the restaurant?' I say. Talking of "putty in the hands" it seems a logical progression.

Sid looks glum. 'Yeh. She's got this diabolical creep called Renato who does his stuff in her wine bars. You know she's got this thing about eye-ties?'

I nod understandingly. Not just eye-ties. Anything south of Beachy Head gets her going. If you came from the Isle of Wight and had a sun tan you would stand a good chance with our Rosie.

'He's going to look after it,' says Sid. 'He wants to call it the "Casa Romantica". Did you ever hear anything like it?'

'Should get them going, Sid. The only thing is that I don't reckon Italian grub fits in with the slimming kick. Once they get past the age of consent you don't see a lot of skinny Italian birds about. They're usually standing round the village pump fingering their jowls.'

'You tell Rosie that,' says Sid. 'She and her precious Renato can sort it out. You talk to them when you're down there.'

He tells me that I have two days to meet the rest of the staff and learn the ropes. Sidney would like to give me a personal tour but he has 'important matters to attend to', so my introduction to Beauty Manor is going to be undertaken by Mr Roughage.

'He's very good at handling staff,' explains Sid and I have the evidence of my own minces to support this statement.

I am quite looking forward to seeing the ancient heap again – I refer to Beauty Manor – and I wonder whether I will bump into Lady Baulkit. It is amazing how quickly even Mum's grub has got me on my feet again. The sack no longer holds any terrors for my action man kit and a spot of steerage through the peerage would not go down amiss.

* * * *

I notice the change that has come over Long Hall immediately. The grass has been cut back so that you can see the fruit trees, and the flowerbeds no longer look like conveyor belts for weeds. Wanda Zonker must have worked wonders to squeeze so much moola out of Sir Henry. I expect that I will be seeing her as well. Sidney suggested that she would be popping in to 'show us the ropes' as he put it.

The front door is open and when I ring the door-bell nobody comes. You would hardly expect them to, would you? Not unless they were kinky about door bells. Anyway, I see an electrician's box on the floor so I reckon he must be on the job somewhere. Not a bad supposition as I find when I look in the drawing room. A white Khyber is bobbing up and down on the rug in front of the fire and beneath it is a bird I have not seen with her skirt up around her waist. The couple do not seem to be aware of my presence so I enjoy the sight for a few minutes before coughing discreetly.

The bird sees me first and nearly chucks the bloke over her shoulder. She pulls down her skirt, scrambles to her feet and curtseys.

'I be the under maid,' she says.

'So I saw,' I say wittily. 'I'm employed by Mr Noggett. Can you tell me where I find Mr Roughage?'

The bloke is scrambling into a pair of blue overalls behind the settee and he nods down the corridor.

'I think he be in the pantry,' he says. 'There won't be any trouble, will there?' The bird looks at me with pleading eyes and I consider her trim little body and firm inviting breasts.

'I hope not,' I say giving the judy a look rich in meaning e.g. I'll play ball with you, if you play with my balls.

I leave the once happy couple to decide whether it it worth getting on the job again and nip down to where I remember the kitchen being. A contented groaning noise suggests that I may have found the right spot and, remembering Mr Roughage's delicate heart condition, I apply my bottle to the Rory rather than risk causing further damage by barging in.

'It's a devil, you are, Mr Roughage,' says a voice with more than a hint of the blarney in it. 'It's the last time I'll ever bend over to reach the bottom of the biscuit barrel.'

A glance through the keyhole is enough to reveal her predicament – not to mention a few other parts of her body not usually seen bent double on the front cover of *House Beautiful*. The staff are certainly on good terms with each other at Beauty Manor. It will be interesting to see whether the mood of practising together catches on with the paying guests.

Mr Roughage seems to be in no mood to bring his business to a speedy conclusion so I decide to have a wander round the house and see if I can catch up with any more of my old friends. At least I will be able to have a gander at some of the alterations. I have hardly had time to admire the new black and white checkered tiles in the hallway than I hear the sound of angry voices coming from the landing.

'You filthy foreign slut!'

'How dare you talk to me like that! You see what she thinks of foreigners, Renato?'

'Eez nota vera nice, Rosie.'

Oh well, Guinness and light can't last for ever as the poet says. Two of the voices are well known to me and the other is less difficult to pick out than a hashamite's hampton at a toad stool convention.

'Hello, Rosie,' I sing out in my best 'stop the bull and cow' voice.

'Oh, it's you.' Rosie sounds less excited than Ted Heath watching a bedraggled Harold Wilson struggle over the side of his yacht. Not very encouraging when you think how long it is since we have seen each other. Still she obviously has other things on her mind.

Both Wanda and Renato are wearing dressing gowns and flushed expressions and it seems possible that Rosie might have caught them in full Balaclava. Should Rosie have more than a professional interest in Renato this could obviously have caused distress. Rosie can get very worked up. I remember how she used to burst into tears if anyone ever said anything nasty about Sid. As you can imagine, she had furrows down her cheeks.

'You know Miss Wonky?'

'Zonker!!'

'I have had the pleasure,' I say.

Rosie sniffs. 'That wouldn't surprise me. The woman is insatiable.'

'She's Lithuanian,' I correct her.

Rosie looks at me in a funny way and turns to Renato. 'I employ you to run the restaurant, not have it off with – with the staff.'

'I beg your pardon,' says Wanda. 'I'm in charge here. Signor Ronaldi comes under me.'

This seems a distinct possibility and I can see the same thought occurring to Rosie. Fortunately, the maestro speaks.

'I think I go and discharge my beeziness,' he says. He snakes off before anyone can find out what he means. I am not certain I want to know, anyway.

Wanda and Rosie bristle before each other. I can see that the presence of these two powerful and headstrong women could form a source of future problems for Inches Limited. Rosie does not like taking things lying down – as anybody who walked past the front porch of 17 Scraggs Lane in the old days could have told you – and Wanda is no slouch in the dynamism department.

'How about a nice cup of yourself?' I say diplomatically to Rosie – Rosie Lea, tea, see?

'I've got to be getting back to London,' she says all hoity-toity like. 'Come, Timothy. I want a word with you.'

I smile pleasantly at Wanda who ignores me and pad after Rosie.

'Are you going to come down often?' I ask nervously.

'Not more than I can help,' says my only sister. 'I want you to keep an eye on my investment. I have a large stake in this place.'

'In the deep freeze, is it?' I say. 'I hope the electricity is on because the bloke who—'

'Not that kind of steak, Timmy! Don't you ever change? You're dimmer than you were when we were all at home.'

'I think I'm sweet the way I am,' I say. 'You don't always change for the best, you know.'

'Is that a crack at me?' says Rosie.

'No, not especially,' I say, realising that I am getting into deep water. 'But you have changed, haven't you? I mean, the boutiques and the wine bars and all that. I remember when Sid got that flat in Streatham. You thought you were in Buckingham Palace.'

'That's the last thing he got though, isn't it? If it hadn't been for me we wouldn't be where we are now.'

'Where are you now, Rosie?'

Rosie stops patting her barnet in the large mirror in the hall and turns to face me.

'What do you mean?'

I shrug my shoulders. It is very difficult talking to your sister like this. It would be much easier with a mate or someone you hardly knew.

'You seemed to be much happier when you first married. You didn't have much but it didn't seem to matter. Now you're well off you never see each other and you want more all the time. You never relax.'

Rosie looks round the hall. 'I'm afraid that's life,' she says. 'Very few people stay the same.'

'Sid hasn't changed a lot,' I say.

Rosie squeezes my arm and it reminds me that she used to be a great toucher and cuddler. 'That says it all, doesn't it? You know, and I know, that Sid is never going to change. When we got married I didn't know that. I didn't know that I was going to change. You never do.'

'What about Renato?' When I say it, I wish I hadn't.

'Don't ask too many personal questions, Timmy.' She gives my arm another squeeze. 'We both know that Sidney is no saint.'

'Yeah, but. . . .' My voice tails away.

'He was like that right from the beginning,' says Rosie, firmly. 'It used to amuse me the way he thought I didn't know.'

We both stand there saying nothing. I don't know why we are having this conversation because we each know what the other one is thinking and we know that it isn't going to change anything. Rosie walks away waving her hand.

'Look out for Wonky,' she says. And then, almost as an afterthought, 'Wait till you get married.'

In the old days I would have said 'Oh no. Not me. I'm not going to get married.' But now it seems almost inevitable. Like losing your Teds. Or your barnet rushing down the back of your nut. It doesn't seem any more pleasant a prospect – quite the reverse when you take a gander about you – but I know it's going to happen.

I can count the number of birds I have brought home on the embarrassing experiences of one lifetime; but in the old days Mum used to give them her 'you're not good enough for my boy' butcher's the minute they set foot on the door-step. She always looked at them as if they'd trodden dog shit into the carpet. Now they get a cup of tea, and a piece of cake if they're really unlucky. She's practically bolting out of the door to put up the banns. Even Dad has been known to comment favourably on what marriage has done for Sid. Still, with Dad's mentality he would probably reckon that Dartmoor was a good idea because it taught you to sew.

I am cogitating on such matters – it's all right, it doesn't stunt your growth – when I find myself looking into the bed-room I once shared with Lady Baulkit. What a lovely woman she was when stripped to the buff. That black choker round her neck, the reflections in the mirror above the bed, Whhhhhhhhh! It is enough to give your action man kit a crick in the knackers. There must be something about this place because everyone seems to get on the job the minute they get over the threshold – or flesh-hold as it ought to be called.

I sit down on the Uncle Ned and gaze out of the burnt cinders at a prospect of distant trees. It fair brings tears to the minces. How different from my pent house suite in Scraggs Lane. There you have to go out on the landing to open the cupboard door – and I mean the cupboard in the room! There wouldn't be space to swing a cat even if it touched toes.

Overcome by nostalgia – no, it is not a pain in the head – I lie back and close my eyes. As is often the case with me, I then open them again. Swimming in the mirror above my head is the reflection of a bird. A bird I at first take for Lady Baulkit. Hoping for a nice surprise, I sit up quickly. It is not Lady Baulkit. The judy examining me like a run in a new pair of tights bears a striking resemblance to Sir Henry's old lady but is much younger.

'You're one of them, I suppose?' she says ripping off the words like they are the last sheets of a roll of Bronco and she has just won a prune eating contest.

'I beg your pardon,' I say. 'These trousers just happened to shrink in the wash.'

'I meant, you must be one of the health farm crowd.' She might be chipping the words off the side of a glacier.

'That's right,' I say. 'Timothy Lea. I'm Mr Nogget's assistant.' I am trying to sound all nice and friendly but she keeps her voice packed in ice cubes.

'I don't know any of the people involved,' she says. 'I only know what my mother has told me.'

'Lady Baulkit is your mum, is she?' I say, showing that I catch on fast.

"Mum" is only a three letter word but it goes through Lady B.'s little girl like a bullet.

'You have ascertained the relationship,' she says, wincing.

'I've met your father too,' I say. 'He's one of the directors isn't he?'

'My father is a director of lots of companies. Most of them insolvent as far as I can make out. Quite what characterises his business judgement I find it impossible to fathom.'

'Yes,' I say, not certain what she is on about.

'I sometimes give up a grateful prayer that he was not alive at the time of the South Sea Bubble.'

'Indeed,' I say. Now she has really got me. I presume she is rabbiting about a Bubble and Squeak or Beak. Beak meaning, of course, a Once-a-Week or magistrate. I recall that there was a coloured geezer who sat at the South London Magistrates Court but he came from Ceylon or Typhoo, or somewhere like that. I don't know whether you call that the South Seas. Of course, it might be that she is talking about a Bubble and Squeak or Greek, but that seems less likely, somehow. I do wish people would make themselves clear.

Miss Baulkit's face softens a fraction. 'I'm sorry if I sound rather abrupt,' she says. 'It's not your fault, I suppose. If I want to complain to anybody I should be talking to my father. He's the one who's handed over the house.'

'This is the first time you've seen all the changes, is it?' Miss B. shudders. 'The place looks like a sanatorium. All those ghastly machines. I had no idea it was going on. I only came back from finishing school yesterday.'

'I haven't seen it all myself, yet,' I say. 'You finished school for good, have you?'

I don't have time to prolong our rabbit because Wanda Zonker appears in the doorway. She is wearing a leotard and looking efficient.

'Ah. There you are, Timothy. I want you to come with me, please.'

I have a feeling that she wants to get a grip of me, just to show that being Rosie's brother does not count for anything and that she is still the boss. Oh dear. I hope I am not going to be ground to pieces between two forceful personalities.

Lady Baulkit's bricks and mortar is standing beside the bed as I leave the room. The sunlight picks out the highlights in her long blonde barnet and splashes onto the counterpane and in this setting so rich in memory and historical association I feel something that it is almost impossible to convey in words. Sheer, naked lust comes some way towards it but it is more complicated than that. I would like to give her one – but nicely. I wonder if it is more than mere coincidence that has thrown us together at a point when I was thinking about getting dot and carried? I have always fancied the English rose type for breeding purposes and Miss Baulkit's initial resistance to my obvious charms is also a turn on. Any bird that has the good taste to find me repellant automatically excites interest. No doubt she is staying with mum at the dower house so I will see some more of her. I wonder if the title can be passed on by the female members of the line? Probably only the clap as with most families.

While I am deciding what to have for my coat of arms – a

couple of large bristols with a hampton rampant seems favourite – I am following Miss Zonker down the long corridor that leads towards the back of the house. Willowing along in her black leotard she looks like a plastic hour glass and I recall favourably our spot of in and out in Chapter One. Could it be that she has another pubic rampage in mind? I must say that the idea is more appealing than a weekend spent scouring Harold Wilson's teeth.

'Here we are,' she says, throwing open a door. 'The Kung Fu massage class. I've found you a model, Miss Nishi.'

Miss Nishi is quite dishy and obviously nippon through and through – either that or Gordon Banks in drag. She is wearing a kimono and standing beside a sunken bath. Around it are grouped half a dozen fanciable birds wearing togas – you know, what the Romans used to wear before the invention of fly buttons. They are all British and, I reckon, local maidens recruited by Roughage. I deduct that from the fact that one of them is still chewing a straw and another moving her hands up and down as if milking a cow.

'Ah so,' says Miss Nishi, bowing her nut. 'Grateful so much. Remove clothes and lie in bath, please.'

'I will leave you in Miss Nishi's capable hands,' says Wanda.

'Hang on a minute—!' I say, but she has scarpered. The girls press forward revealing signs of interest.

'Please. There is little time to instil art.' Miss Nishi waves me towards the bath. 'No need to feel shame. Japanese proud of body.' She unties the sash at her waist and pulls open her kimono. She is a bit broad in the fife but quite a nice little number. She also has a heart-shaped muff which would be nice on St Valentine's day – probably quite nice on any other day as well.

'But I—'

'Girls. You will assist, please.'

Before you say 'get em orf!' six pairs of Germans are interfering with my clothing to the point of stripping me stark bollock naked. You can imagine what I feel – plenty.

'Now, in bath please.'

There does not seem much point in having a barney about it so I climb into the bath and lie down. I don't mind the birds looking at me but I wish they would look at my face.

'Now, watch closely. I take soap so, and apply to body.' I think she means my body but not a bit of it. She starts to lather herself up something arousing. It may make her clean but it makes me feel very dirty. Oh dear, I wish I had more control over percy. He is a dead embarrassment to me at moments like this – not so much of the dead, either. Tower Bridge could pick up a few tips.

'Now, girls. All take off tunics and imitate – I say "imitate", Ruby!'

I am glad she pointed that out. I thought I was going to have to blush for a moment. Some of these country birds look as if they would go off like a tin of pre-war snoek. I suppose it is watching the animals. My Aunty Edna had a very nasty experience with a keeper in the monkey house at the zoo.

I watch them tugging off their togas and it occurs to me that this Kung Fu massage is a bit unusual. I mean, you would not get it on the National Health, would you? Not even with Labour in. Not, of course, that I have got anything yet, but I can't help thinking that there must be more to it than lying on your back and watching a load of birds strip down to the buff and rub themselves with Band of Hope. I am proved right.

'Now, Watch closely.' You could hear a pin drop. 'Kung Fu!!' Quick as a flasher, Miss Nishi leaps down into the bath and chucks herself on top of me. I am so surprised I don't know what to do. The bird does not stay still but glides up and down like she is planing a piece of wood. How immodest! I don't know where to put my face – not that I have much choice, Miss Nishi is swamping it with her bristols.

'Notice, please. Rotation of hips very important.'

Gordon Bennett! How is a normal red-blooded Englishman supposed to respond to this treatment? Miss Nishi goes over me like a carpet shampooer and there are more suds than you see in a washing up liquid ad on the telly – sort of hell for lather, if you get my meaning.

'Kung Fu massage improve muscle control. Note how model's toes curl and belly rigid.'

My Darby Kelly is not the only thing! A strange shape is rising from the sea of foam and it is a penis not Venus. Percy has never known anything like it. My whole body feels as if an electric current is being passed through it and I have to close my eyes against the waves of ecstasy – and the soap. What Miss Nishi is doing with her hands is somebody's business as well. You saw 'Gidgit goes Hawaiian'? Well this is 'Digits go Haywire'. I am in danging of losing my deposit. Just in time, Miss Nishi rolls to one side and the crisis is averted.

'Now. You see how is done. And Ruby. You shout "Kung Fu" not "Fuck You!" You understand?"

Ruby nods. She is a large bird with knockers like a couple of sacks of porridge.

'It be like mangel wurzle festival at Farmer Trimball's,' she says. 'They stick their mangel wurzle's through the holes in the fence and—'

'Silence please!' demands Miss Nishi.

'You can make do with a turnip,' says Ruby.

'And now I seek volunteer – I say volunteer!!'

But she says it too late. The birds are whipping themselves into a lather before you can say 'Loved him, hated hernia'. Ruby does not even wait for the soap before launching herself on top of me. My, but she is a big girl. So big that it is impossible to avoid your Marquis of Lorne slipping into her grumble and grunt.

It does not stay there for long because another charmer grabs a piece of the action – and another – and another. Soon the scene must look like a colony of seals after a shipload of detergent has sunk off their island. The last thing I see before I pass out is Miss Nishi's face beaming down at me.

'Velly good,' she says. 'And now I show you Karate Caress!!'

## CHAPTER 7

In which Mum and Dad visit Beauty Manor and take lunch with Timmy and Lady Baulkit's attractive daughter, Clarissa. The meal is not a success.

I can't remember what happened during the Karate Caress so I suppose I must still have been out for the count – as opposed to being out for the cunt which is more normally the case. All I know is that after that session in the Kung Fu Massage Chamber my dick has about as much appetite for living as a homeless welk. If that is the standard treatment meted out to clients I reckon they are going to need a heart transplant machine as well as all the other gadgets. And why does Miss Zonker keep popping up with her camera? I must talk to Sidney about it.

But when Sidney rolls up he has other things on his mind. Lots of them. The guests are arriving and a line of swank limousines wait impatiently to get close enough to the front door to disgorge their passengers and mountains of luggage. They seem pretty much the same as the lot at Bosky Dell. Fat businessmen clutching wafer thin brief cases and fat women weighed down with furs and jewellery.

Sid looks at them and shakes his head. 'You know I mentioned to your mum and dad about coming down here?'

'Yes, Sid.'

'Well they want to come. Diabolical, isn't it? I only asked them because I thought they wouldn't want to. People have no bleeding tact, do they?'

'Very dicey, Sid,' I say. 'They're going to stick out here like a sore nunga. And talking of sore nungas—'

'I don't want to, Timmy. Slap some vaseline on it and leave me to concentrate on running this place. My whole future is wrapped up in it. When your parents show up, I want you to look after them. This place is supposed to be dead couth. I can just see your Dad nausing everything up if he gets half a chance. Keep him out of the way. Keep them both out of the way.'

'All right! All right!' I say. 'You bleeding invited them.' I am not overjoyed to hear that Mum and Dad are coming, either. I hardly feel that their presence is going to help my relationship with Clarissa – yeh, that is the Baulkit bird's name. Dead posh.

Please don't think that I am ashamed of my parents. It is just that they do have habits which some people find it difficult to adjust to. The light went out with Linda Figgis when Dad borrowed her brooch to prise out a grape stone that had got stuck in his dentures. Mind you, he did spread his handkerchief over his knee before he did it. He is not totally without refinement.

Roughage is responsible for staff organization and goosing and he assigns me to the Kleinhausen volcanic mud machine.

'It's very simple,' he says. 'You pour the mud in here and it shoots out of all these holes under pressure. The customer standing in the cabinet is bombarded with hot mud.'

'Why?' I say.

'Because it costs three guineas a throw, that's why,' says Roughage, testily. 'Don't ask silly questions.'

'Where does the volcanic mud come from?'

'The shores of Lake Tanzania.'

'Blimey! That's a bit far, isn't it?'

'No. It's about two fields away. Mr Noggett named it the other day. You'd better grab a couple of buckets and get over there.'

'Thanks a lot,' I say. Blooming nice, isn't it? All my management potential and I end up filling buckets with mud. I could have got a better job down the beg o' my neighbour.

'One thing you'll have to be careful of,' says Roughage, 'don't turn the control past where the needle goes into the red area when there is anyone in the cabinet. That passes steam through the system and is only used for scouring the apparatus.'

'Don't!' I say. 'I get prickles up my spine just thinking about it. Why is it on wheels?'

'So you can move it around and plug it in anywhere. The manufacturers speak very highly of it. Look what it says in the brochure: "Once the pleasure it has been enjoyed. Never far away from it you will want to be."'

'Olé!' I say. 'I'm still a bit worried about it all, Mr Roughage. I mean, this must be a highly technical piece of machinery. The clients are going to realise that I know next to nothing about it.'

'No they won't. Not if you don't let them. Remember, they won't have seen one either. Kleinhausen were making parts for supersonic aircraft until recently.'

But I am still worried as I trip across the meadows with my buckets. I wish I had been assigned to something else. Anything except Miss Nishi and her helpmates. I still get a twinge in my tonk just thinking about that.

'Whooh, Henry!!' A shrill neigh assaults my lug holes and through the willows crash a horse and rider. I have hardly had time to register the upper class rabbit than the mighty beast rears up and paws the air with its hooves.

Before you can say 'Hi ho, Tonto, and away!' Clarissa Baulkit has parted company with her mount and landed in an attractive pile at my feet – fortunately she misses the very unattractive pile a couple of feet away.

The high-spirited Henry thunders away into the trees shaking its backside gleefully.

'Damn that nag!' says Clarissa slapping her jodphurs with her crop. 'They'll be no stopping him till nightfall, now.'

'Are you all right?' I say. 'You took a nasty tumble.'

'Only my pride is hurt,' says the plucky little creature. 'If that brute doesn't learn some obedience I'm going to have him gelded.'

'It'll make him easier to see in the dark, I suppose,' I say.

'What are you talking about?' Says Clarissa impatiently.

'Painting the horse gold,' I say.

'Oh, God! I said gelded not gilded!'

When she looks at me like that – her eyes full of contempt – I really fancy her. A spot of upper class good taste goes a long way with me.

She takes a step and winces. 'Dammit! I think I've twisted an ankle.'

'I'll give you a hand,' I say. 'I was supposed to be fetching some mud for the Kleinhausen Volcanic Mud Machine but that can wait.'

'For ever, I should think,' sniffs the fair Clarissa. 'What a damn nuisance. I was jogging over to Melton Hall for a spot of tiffin.'

I imagine this must be some upper class game like polo. No need to feel ashamed that I have not participated.

'I've never tiffed,' I say.

'Oh no!' Clarissa closes her eyes and I imagine that she must be in real pain. Maybe because I have clocked her with one of the buckets. I had better put them down. 'Lunch!' she shrieks. 'Lunch!'

What a good idea. I can take her into the 'Karsi Romantica', or whatever it is called and get her all worked up over a plate of spaghetti and chips. With a bit of luck I might even be able to get it buckshee. After all she is the daughter of one of the directors.

'I would be honoured to offer you dinner in the new resturant,' I say. 'I believe it's very good if you like wop food.'

'A drink is what I need at the moment,' says Clarissa reacting with desire-enhancing cool to my suggestion. 'I'll worry about food later.'

I help her hobble back to the house and, as promised, she makes straight for the bazaar. She has a large Mahatma Gandhi to pull herself together and though I fancy a pint of apple fritter I have to settle for Gunga Din because there is not an Aristotle of pig's ear in the Mickey Mouse. I don't really mind because I need a bit of courage and I always reckon that I get Mozart faster on spirits.

We have another one and by this time she has no alternative but to stay for dinner. She goes off to phone her mate and I nip into the resturant to tell Renato the good news. He may be giving my sister one but he seems a nice bloke and eager to oblige.

'Leava everythinga to mea,' he says. 'I willa impregnate you myself.'

'I think you mean serve,' I say, wondering what kind of book he learnt his English out of. Probably one of those ones you can get from Battersea Public Library with all the diagrams torn out.

I bring Clarissa to the table and have just offered her a bread stick when I hear a voice that makes my Newingtons turn to Neptune's daughter.

'Timothy! Thank Gawd you're here. Got fifty riddle, have you? You wouldn't cocoa how much it cost to take a bleeding taxi from the station. I told your mother we should have waited for the bus but you know what she's like. Thinks I'm bleeding made of money.'

Where my mother could have got such an impression from is a mystery to me, but that is not the main thought that is occupying my mind. As Dad wipes his forehead with Clarissa's serviette I can see my chances of making headway with Lady Baulkit's daughter disappearing up the spout. No amount of suavity on my part is going to compensate for his presence. I had thought of introducing them after we were married.

'Here's 50p, Dad,' I say. 'Oh, and this is Clarissa Baulkit.'

'Wotcha,' says Dad. 'I hope you know what you're letting yourself in for, knocking around with this berk. Going steady, are you?'

'Certainly not!' Clarissa turns approximately half as scarlet as I am.

'Good thinking,' says Dad. 'What's the nosh like here?' He does not wait for an answer but taps a distinguished looking geezer sitting near us on the shoulder. 'Is that all right, mate?'

'This man is your father?' says Clarissa. You sense that she is not automatically drawn to him.

'In a manner of speaking,' I say.

While Clarissa shudders, Mum comes into the restaurant.

'Come on!' she says to Dad. 'He's doing his nut out there. He thinks you've scarpered.' They must be able to hear her in the sauna bath. Oh dear. How humiliating it all is.

'Belt up and sit down,' says Dad. 'We'll have some nosh with Timmy and his girl friend. Nice canteen they've got here, isn't it?'

'I'm not sitting down till I've washed my hands,' says Mum all posh-like. She has the savoy fear to respond to her surroundings like me, you see.

'Why? You haven't done anything with them,' says Dad.

'Mum, this is Clarissa,' I say.

'Pleased to meet you, dear,' says Mum. 'I've always said it was time our Timmy found a nice girl and settled down. Been horse riding, have you?'

'I thought she was a land girl,' says Dad.

'You're not still here, are you?' says Mum. 'Piss off and pay that taxi.'

She and Dad go there separate ways and I wonder why fate has got it in for me. I have always helped old ladies across the road and been kind to animals.

'You ava mada decision?' Renato is holding his little pad up underneath his chin.

I feel like telling him that I have decided to cut my throat but he would not understand, poor sod.

'I thinka you lika the gamberoni.'

He is dead right of course but it is not the kind of thing you want to talk about when you are taking a bird out for the first time.

'I'll have the lasagne and the veal,' says Clarissa shoving her menu firmly into Renato's mit.

'Si, bella signorina. And for the signior?'

'That's just what I was going to have,' I say. 'Isn't that a coincidence? Do you fancy anything to start with?'

'I was going to have the lasagne to start with!' snaps Clarissa.

'Good idea,' I say. Bloody eyeties! They have to make it difficult for you, don't they? It only needs Clarissa to realise that I am a trifle out of my depth and I will be really in the shit.

'Right, lads. Eyes down for the count up.' Dad plonks himself down besides Clarissa and tucks his serviette in the front of his cardigan. I have not seen him in such a good mood for years. It must be the thought of cashing in on some free grub. 'What do you fancy, mother?' he says. 'That bloke's spaghetti looked all right. Hey, Beppo. Multo spaghettio multo quicko or you'll collect a kick up the khyber.'

Renato bows respectfully and hurries away.

'No need to talk to him like that,' says Mum. 'We had a very nice Italian man who used to come round with onions hanging all over him.'

'He was French!' says Dad contemptuously. 'Blimey. Anybody knows it's the frogs who wear those little cow pats with a pimple in the middle.'

This enlightening conversation is interrupted by the reappearance of Renato. 'You lika something to drinka?'

'Oh yes.' I pick up the wine list and try to find something I can pronounce.

Renato looks at Clarissa, lowers his voice and winks. 'I think the bella signorina finda the sixty-nina very pleasant.'

He doesn't mind what he says, does he? I don't mind the bloke being friendly but when he starts giving me advice on my sex life that is too much. I can now see why there is a cover charge mentioned at the top of the menu. These geezers would cover anything for 25p.

'I'll have this one,' I say jabbing my shaking finger at the list.

'Agua minerale? Certainly, Signior. What you lika? You like Pschitt?'

'Not before the meal, mate,' says Dad. 'What a funny thing to ask. They must do things differently in Wopland.'

He turns to Clarissa. 'Are you feeling comfortable, dear. You don't want to take advantage of the gentleman's offer? You're probably better to hang on to it if you can. They got different standards of hygiene to us in these hot countries.'

'Dad. Please! I'm certain he didn't mean that.'

'I'd like a bottle of wine. Valpolicella. And please, make it fast.' Clarissa speaking.

'They make it on the premises, do they?' says Mum. 'That is interesting. I always thought you had to leave it for a bit.'

I dare not look at Clarissa. What a disaster. What must she think? I know I come from the wrong side of the tracks as far as she is concerned but now it looks as if you have to take a bus ride when you get to the other side.

'It's a nice place this, isn't it?' says Dad. 'They've done it up nice, too. Don't you reckon?'

'Since I was born and raised here, I find it difficult to adjust to the new decor,' sniffs Clarissa. 'Possibly this is a failing in myself as it would never have entered my mind that anyone could attempt to blend orange and purple.'

'I think it's rather cheery,' says Mum. 'Especially with the plaid tablecloths.'

'Lasagne?' says the waiter.

'I don't know, mate. I'm a stranger here myself,' says Dad.

'Here,' says Clarissa.

'Oh, you mean the bread and butter pudding,' says Dad, watching the plate that is dumped in front of Clarissa. 'Why didn't you say so?'

'You lika cheese?' says the waiter with half a nervous eye on Dad.

'Don't be stupid!' says Dad. 'We no have sugar on bread and butter pudding. You savvy, Benvenuto?' Dad is speaking very slowly on his best talking-to-foreigners voice.

'Really!' Clarissa looks as if she is going to do her nut at any moment. 'This isn't bread and butter pudding. It's pasta.'

'Oh yeah? Let's have a look.' Dad picks up a menu. 'Oh

I see. Like our fish paste, is it? I don't fancy it, whatever it is. I'm glad I stuck to the spaghetti. Here—' He nudges Clarissa in the ribs so that her first mouthful of grub flops onto her blouse. '—be a laugh if I did, wouldn't it? You know, got stuck to my spaghetti.'

'Have some wine, Dad,' I say.

'In a minute, son. I'll just help this lady clean herself up. Our Timmy was a messy eater when he was a kiddy, you know.'

'Please! I can rub it myself, thank you.' What Dad has been doing to the front of Clarissa's blouse would get an X Certificate in Greater London. Gawd, but he is a disgusting old man! This must put the kibosh on my romance.

'Hurry up with the spaghetti, mate. My guts are beginning to grumble.' Dad grabs a waiter who is passing behind him and half a dozen plates crash to the floor.

'Control yourself!' scolds Mum. 'Timmy and his girl friend are having an ordoover.'

'I thought they were having a lozenga,' says Dad. 'Ah, here it comes. Crash the vino, Timmy.' He gives Clarissa another nudge.

'This is like Christmas, isn't it, darling?'

'It seems more like the Day of Atonement to me,' groans Clarissa.

'Yeh, that's very true,' says Dad. 'Right, Beppo. Slap it down there, lad, and let's get stuck into it.'

When Dad says 'get stuck into it' he is not kidding. It is quite disgusting what he does to that spaghetti. All the loose ends are hanging out of his cakehole and there are bits dropping down and spattering his serviette. I see Clarissa take a quick gander at him and wince.

'Give us some more wine, Timmy. It's a nice drop of stuff this. What is it, Sainsbury's?'

Dad drinks like he is draining the plonk through his teeth and his glass is full of bits of spaghetti. Its rim looks like a pony's mouth after a hard canter.

Renato appears carrying a bowl of beans. 'You lika fagio-lini?' he says.

'Don't be personal,' says Dad.

'Thank you,' says Clarissa and Renato dumps some beans on her plate.

Renato turns to Dad and nods towards his plate. 'And Signior. You lika a bit on the sida?'

'How dare you!' Dad lumbers to his feet and the wine bottle falls over and glugs onto Clarissa's riding breeches. 'What a question to ask a man in front of his family. You want to watch your language, Mussolini. Remember who won the war. We don't have to put up with your lot over here. Enoch Powell isn't going to stay in the wilderness for ever, you know.'

'Dad! Please—!'

Clarissa stands up. 'I'm sorry, I must go. I can't stand any more.'

'Now see what you've done!' storms Dad. 'Don't you go, girl. Don't let them push you around. You sit down for your rights.'

'I'm going because of you, you odious moron!!!' shouts Clarissa.

'See!? She's distraught. You've got her all hysterectical, you greasy, foul-mouthed dago!'

So saying, Dad picks up his plate of spaghetti and heaves it in Renato's mush. Renato does not take kindly to this and proceeds to strangle Dad across the table. It is a pity because all the bread sticks get broken.

'I'm sorry about this,' I say to Clarissa. 'Perhaps we can have dinner another time. Was your las-los-starter nice?' But she has already gone.

# CHAPTER 8

In which Dad interferes with both Mrs Bevcole and the Kleinhausen Volcanic Mud Machine. A course of action that has distressing results for both.

I am very upset by Dad's uncouth behaviour and Sidney does his nut.

'Bloody marvellous!' he says. 'He's hardly walked through the front door and he's nearly wrecked the place. And what about the effect on the guests? They were going spare in my office.'

'Serve them right,' I say. 'They should be concentrating on their diets.'

'No they shouldn't!' snarls Sid. 'They should be concentrating on spending money. Why do you think the restaurant is situated opposite the steam cabinets?'

'So you can cook fish in them?'

'No, you stupid berk! So the punters are tempted when they're at their weakest. Gordon Bennett! You and your Dad. What a pair!'

'Yes,' I say. I am agreeing with Sid's last remark in as far as it aptly describes the set of knockers that have just loomed up behind his left shoulder. Fortunately for my peace of mind they are surrounded by a nice looking bird of about 38–26–38 and not drifting about by themselves.

'Is there anybody on duty in the mud room?' she says. 'I'm dying to have a go on that German thing.'

'Certainly, modom,' says Sid, putting on his best 'step this way' voice. 'The assistant is here.' He grabs me by the arm and hisses into my ear-hole. 'Pull yourself together! And that meal is coming out of your wages.'

'What wages?' I say.

'Precisely!' snaps Sid. He turns to the bird. 'Here we are, Mrs Bevcole. Your assistant awaits.'

I am feeling really choked as I follow Mrs Bevcole upstairs. Even the thought of feasting my minces on her shapely limbs does little to compensate for my humiliation in front of Clarissa Baulkit. Clarissa Baulkit! The words trip off the tongue like Accles and Pollock or Bangers and Mash. They are beautiful. How tragic that they may never be linked with mine. Clarissa Lea. Now there is a poem for you in two words. Must I really face up to the fact that we can never be one? As the possibility becomes fainter so my desire becomes stronger. I will not surrender hope. Faith can move mountains and the municipal piss house at the end of Scraggs Lane only got through after the second planning application.

'I'll put on my robe and see you there,' says Mrs B. 'It's quite safe, isn't it?'

'Of course,' I say. 'Safe as houses.' I remember those words later.

I have slipped into my toga and am on the way to the Kleinhausen Volcanic Mud Machine when I suddenly remember that I did not get any mud for the thing. Knickers! I wait for Mrs B. in the treatment room and tell her to hang on while I draw some from the storeroom.

'It's so precious, we don't leave it lying about,' I say.

I streak down the corridor – you know what I mean – and bump into Mum.

'Have you seen your father?' she says.

'If I had there would be blood on my hands,' I say. 'Why? What's happened to the rotten old sod? Nothing harmless, I hope.'

'He's disappeared,' says Mum. 'Oh dear. I do hope there's not going to be trouble. You know what he's like when he's had a few.'

'What do you mean, "trouble"?' I say. 'What do you think that was back in the restaurant? Half a ton of crockery smashed, two black eyes and a broken nose, one bird with hysterics, my relationship with Clarissa up the spout. Blimey! Doesn't that sound like trouble?'

'Yes, dear. It must have been trying for you, but—'

'I'm sorry Mum. I don't have time. If you see him, lock him in your room for gawd's sake.'

I don't fancy leaving the old bleeder wandering about, but what can I do? Tote that barge, lift that bale, if I don't get the mud I'll be kicked up the tail.

I dash out of the back of the house and start legging it past the stables. The spot where I left the buckets is a couple of hundred yards away and the pond that far again. Maybe I would be better off forgetting about Lake Tanzania and finding something nearer home. I dash into the stables and nearly fall over a couple having it away in the hay.

'Mr Roughage!' Blimey, doesn't the bloke ever do anything else? 'Have you got a spade around here?' I ask.

'There's been some talk about Dolly Cranker,' says Roughage, calmly. 'Her mother used to go to a lot of dances at the U.S.A.F. base. They always said she'd come to no good.'

'Not that kind of spade! I mean a shovel.'

'Round the back,' says the bird who I remember being on the job with the electrician. She certainly leads a busy social life. 'I think I saw one there.'

'Thank you,' I say.

'Don't mention it,' says Roughage. He is an ill-mannered sod. He does not even stop when I am talking to him.

I whizz round the back and hit a bit of luck at last. A bloke is walking along with two buckets.

'Mud?' I say.

'Night soil,' he says. Couldn't be better, could it? Soil is the same as mud only dryer. If I add a bit of water I'll be away.

'Do you want it?' I say.

The bloke looks a bit puzzled. 'I was going to put it on the dung heap,' he says.

'I need it for a bath,' I say.

Now the bloke looks very puzzled.

'A bath?' He says. 'I've heard of people dunking their feet in it. Rheumatism and all that.'

'No, this is a proper bath,' I say. 'It's squeezed out of a lot of little holes. I haven't got time to talk about it now.'

'I'm glad,' says the bloke.

I stagger off with the buckets and the bloke watches me with a funny expression on his face. It doesn't half niff – the mud I mean – and I am glad when I have struggled up the back stairs to the treatment room.

I open the door and – blimey! I am so surprised I nearly drop my buckets. Mrs Bevcole is stretched out naked on one of the massage tables and Dad, stripped to the underpants, is giving her the once over.

'Dad!'

'Just stepping into the breach, son. Smells as if you stepped in something and all.'

'Is this man an imposter?' says Mrs B. 'I thought some of the things he did were – well, a bit strange.'

This puts me in a spot, because if I say 'yes' I will be in dead stuck. I had better fall back on my proven powers of tact and diplomacy.

'Oh no,' I say. 'Mr Lea has been doing this kind of thing for years.' I switch my eye to Dad who is swaying backwards and forwards. 'Be so kind as to help me prepare the machine, Mr Lea.'

'What are you pouring horse shit into it for?' asks Dad.

Mrs Bevcole starts looking alarmed all over again.

'It's not – er that.' I say. 'It's Lake Tanzania mud. It has many beneficial properties as you well know.' I smile reassuringly at Mrs B. and drag Dad behind the machine. 'Pull yourself together you stupid old git!' I hiss. 'You'll have us all out on our ear if you're not careful.'

'Do I get in the cabinet now?' says Mrs B.

'Hang on, darling. I'll open the door for you.' Dad wriggles away from me and nips round the front of the cabinet. Oh my gawd! What a disaster. At least, if she is inside the cabinet she will be out of his reach.

I check that the machine is plugged in and switch on.
'All right?' I say.
'All right,' says Mrs Bevcole.
'All right,' says Dad.
Dad? I come round the front of the machine and – you would not Adam and Eve it, the dirty old devil has got inside with her.
'Get out of there!' I say. There is hardly room for their two heads to stick out of the top and God knows what is happening out of my sight.
'What the—!!' I whip round and there is Sid. 'What are you maniacs doing!?' He screams. 'Turn it off! Turn it off!'
He tries to wrench open the door while I dash round the back and turn the control sharply to the right. A piercing scream suggests that I may have overdone it.
'Help me with this bleeding door!' shouts Sid.
I rush round the front and, in my panic, forget to turn the machine off. Mrs Bevcole is doing her nut but I don't know whether it is because of Dad or the Kleinhausen. Sid and I pull with all our might and something gives. It is the brake that holds the machine in position. There is a blinding flash, and as Sid and I fall flat on our backs, the Kleinhausen trundles out of the door. Smoke and fumes fill the air and when we scramble to our feet and run into the corridor it looks like one of those early steam engines, Stephenson's 'Cock-up' or whatever it was called.
'Help, help!'
'Stop it!'
I think that Mrs Bevcole must now be referring to the progress of the Kleinhausen and I can't blame her for being agitated. It is not very nice, is it? Being pelted with hot horse dung while you are pressed against one of the most horrible herberts in South West London and hurtling towards a marble staircase. Blimey! The staircase!
Sid has seen the danger before me and makes a desperate lunge at the Kleinhausen just as the front wheels flop over the edge. Too late! The machine tears itself from his grasp and

clatters down the steps gathering speed like a toboggan on the Cresta Run. Dad's nut shudders up and down like a piston head. The Kleinhausen starts to spin before it reaches the hallway and the cabinet door bursts open on impact with the marble. Everybody within thirty feet collects a brown overcoat; Dad is flung across the hall and ends up draped over the reception desk. I don't know what happened to his underpants but they are not where you would expect to find them – mind you, it does stretch the imagination trying to conceive of any person who would embark upon a search for them in the first place.

'He-e-e-e-lp!!'

Mrs Bevcole's voice loses a bit of its volume as she hurtles through the front door still accompanied by the Kleinhausen. I close my eyes instinctively and there are shouts of fear and panic followed immediately by a loud crash. Oh my gawd! Dare I look?

I race down the stairs and pick my way carefully to the crowd jostling in the doorway. There, sitting on the steps of his Rolls with the naked Mrs Bevcole in his arms is Sir Henry Baulkit. He looks a little alarmed and very, very angry.

# CHAPTER 9

In which Omar Gord and his fellow oil sheikhs arrive at Beauty Manor and a distressing case of mistaken identity has far reaching consequences.

'So that's what night soil is,' I say. 'Oh dear, I didn't know that. I thought it was like, well, you know, soil. It's a silly name, isn't it?'

'You're a bit silly, yourself,' snarls Sid. 'You and your bleeding father. It's a miracle he hasn't ruined us. When you two team up it's deadly, isn't it? Three hours and the whole place has ground to a halt. Half the clients asking for their money back, the switchboard jammed by newspapermen and solicitors, the staff refusing to clean up the mess – push that bucket over. Gawd, to think I thought I was going to make my fortune out of this place. I should have been circuited.'

'You mean "certified", Sid. "Circuited" means avoided – yeah, maybe you're right.'

'Don't take the piss, Timmo! The time for joking is long past. You got rid of them both, did you?'

I nod. 'I had to give him a bottle of brandy to keep him quiet, though.'

Sid groans. 'Gordon Bennett! Your bleeding Mum and Dad have used up the first month's profits in half a day. If I ever see that old ratbag again I'll swing for him.'

'It was your fault. You asked him.'

I have no sympathy with Sid. He asks for everything he gets. You don't find him slaving his fingers to the bone over a hot steam cabinet. He gets some poor bastard like me to do it. It is a miracle that he is prepared to get down on his hands and knees and help me mop up after the Kleinhausen. The plain truth is that I am the only bloke in the place daft enough to do it – though I draw the line at filling the cracks in the marble with Polyfilla. Sid can be plain barmy sometimes.

'Thank goodness, Wanda knows how to handle Sir Henry,' says Sid. 'If it wasn't for her we'd be right in the shit.'

I am about to inform Sid that that is precisely where we are when I think better of it. You can tell when Sid is in one of his moods. It is at this moment that Roughage appears holding a handkerchief over his hooter.

'Sir Henry wishes to address all members of the staff in the library,' he says coldly. Looking at him it occurs to me that it is one of the few times I have seen him not connected to a member of the opposite sex. It is not a particularly pleasant sight.

'Blimey,' says Sid. 'I spoke too soon.'

But Sir Henry does not want to issue a rocket. He has more important things on his mind. As I look at him in his black jacket and pin stripe trousers it is difficult to imagine what he was doing in that photograph with the two birds. Perhaps he is a nudist in his spare time.

'Right,' he says, leaning back against the huge marble fireplace. 'Thank you all for coming. Now – now – Roughage. Please come and sit over here.' Roughage separates with a bad Grace – she is the parlour maid, I think – and flounces petulantly into the chair indicated by his employer. 'And you.' He is pointing to Renato. 'Stop mixing pasta on your lap. Oh, you're not.'

'Isa spring.' Renato beams round the room and everybody looks the other way. These Italians are like that. Always touching themselves. Have you noticed?

Sir Henry takes a last look round the room and sticks his thumbs in the pockets of his waistcoat.

'Now I am here in a twin capacity as a cabinet minister and a director of Inches Limited and Beauty Manor. What I am going to say affects the whole future of this great country of ours.'

"'era, 'era!' says Renato enthusiastically.

'As you know, this great country of ours is on its knees,

or rather—' Sir Henry holds up his hand in a telling gesture '—on one knee. A position from which we will spring forward to take our true place in history. The reason for us having to take a temporary breathing space is, of course, oil. At the moment we are reliant upon the Arabs for most of our oil supplies.'

It is funny that he should be talking about Arabs because I have just slid an old leather-covered book from one of the shelves. The lettering on the cover is printed in gold and says 'Ye Guide Booke of ye Sexual Actes prepared for ye Arabes' and it is by Sir Richard Lea. I wonder if he was any relation? The bloke inside the cover looks a bit like me but he has a tall, curly brimmed hat, pointed beard and a thing like a Christmas decoration round his neck. It is difficult to be certain.

'Of course, we have our own oil within reach of these islands and before too long we will be reaping the rich harvest of the North Sea.' Sir Henry drones on and I wonder what he is getting at. Cut down on the fuel bills, I suppose. Blimey, it is always the same, isn't it? I can just see him doing without his little creature comforts. 'However, in the short term, there are problems. We must not mortgage our future but we do need to maintain good relations with our suppliers until we are self sufficient. At that moment we can turn to our Arab friends and say—'

'Piss off, wogs!' says Sidney, cheerfully.

' 'Era, 'era!' says Renato.

Sir Henry looks pained. 'That is hardly the language of international diplomacy,' he murmurs.

'Sorry,' says Sid. 'My patriotism carries me away sometimes.'

Sir Henry looks as if he is considering some of the places he would like it to carry Sid to, and then continues. 'It is in relation to this short term end that I am seeking to enlist your co-operation. A trade delegation from the crucial Trucials – I'm sorry.' He manages to spit in Sid's eye when he says 'crucial Trucials'. 'A delegation from a number of important oil producing countries is in this country at the moment. I have invited them here.'

He pauses expectantly and a buzz goes round the room. It is a large bluebottle. Sidney tries to swat it and knocks over a large vase which shatters on the floor. Roughage wakes up.

'I'm sorry,' flaps Sidney. 'I'll get a dust pan and brush.'

Sir Henry calmly holds up a restraining hand. 'Don't bother,' he says. 'It was merely priceless.'

What a marvellous restraint I think to myself. No wonder this country is sliding down the drain with such immense dignity. It makes you proud to be British and skint.

Sid grovels about a bit and then parks his khyber.

'To continue.' At the sound of his master's voice Roughage leans back in his chair and closes his eyes. 'As you all know, Beauty Manor was established not only as a health farm but as a restaurant, convention centre and the best kind of country club. It is in these latter manifestations that I wish you to extend a hand to our Arab friends. Matters of great purport to our country's future will be discussed within these walls. Let it not be said that we did not all play our part.'

'Amen,' says cook.

'I make no secret of the fact that we will be hoping to sign an agreement that will guarantee this country's oil supplies for the next ten vital years. Therefore, everything that you can contribute to the smooth running of the conference and the reception of our guests will be an investment in the future of this sceptered isle.'

'You can rely on us,' says Sid.

'Your fly buttons are undone,' I tell him.

Roughage starts to snore.

'Thank you for your attention,' says Sir Henry. 'When I look round this room and see you all, I know – well, I don't think I have to tell you. You know what I know.'

Everybody nods and wonders what he is on about. When I look round the room I feel like rushing out and buying a packet of candles immediately.

'A very stirring address,' says Sid as we walk down the corridor. He is dabbing his eye with a handkerchief but I think he is still cleaning up after Sir Henry's 'Crucial Trucial'.

I am thinking about Sir Richard Lea, the bloke who taught the Arabs how to put it about. If he is my ancestor this puts a completely different light on my relationship with Clarissa Baulkit. I can expose myself to her as being of noble birth. This should make up for the slight unpleasantness at dinner.

But when I next see Clarissa, I don't have time to chat her up. As Sir Henry's daughter she is put in charge of the arrangements for receiving the guests and the way she goes about it makes the Duke of Norfolk look like Norman Wisdom organising a down tools in a custard pie factory. She is practically examining our finger nails while we wait by the front door.

'Here they come,' says Sid, gazing at a cloud of dust approaching up the drive.

'Surely not,' I say.

'What's she got to do with it?'

'I don't mean Shirley Knot!' I tell the daft sod. 'I mean, surely it's not them coming up the drive. Not in a bus!'

It does not seem likely, does it? Not unless all the oil wells have dried up. In which case we are in dead stuck and can forget about the sheeps' eyes immediately – which is not a second too early for my stomach.

But it is not the big cheeses. It is a bus load of birds wearing long robes and yashmaks. All you can see is their big brown minces giving you the once over.

'Be very careful,' warns Clarissa. 'These women have probably never been out of purdah before.'

'I didn't go abroad until I was twenty-five,' says Sid.

Clarissa looks at him with dull loathing. 'Do nothing to alarm them,' she says.

'No harem scarem,' I say wittily.

Not one flicker of amusement flashes across Clarissa's

mug. She is quite a little Robert Robinson when it comes to splitting your sides. Nevertheless, I love her. That upper class cool really gets me going. I feel that she despises me to the very tips of my toenails and it is a wonderful feeling.

'I wonder when their old men will get here,' says Sid casting a professional eye over the bevy of Eastern beauty.

'In a brace of sheikhs, I expect,' I say.

Clarissa shudders. 'I find your sense of humour insulting,' she says.

Sid proceeds to roll about. 'That's very good,' he says. ' "In sultan". Oh yes, I like that.'

'Shut your mouths, you fools!' snaps my future bride. 'Pull yourselves together and show the ladies to their quarters.'

'Nice bunch of birds these,' says Sid as we shepherd them through the picture gallery. 'I might be crashing the Turkish Delights, later.'

'Sidney!' I hiss. 'How could you with the country's future at stake.'

'You're right,' says Sid. 'I was being immature and not facing up to my responsibilities.'

'That's right,' I say. 'You don't want a blot on your escutcheon, do you?'

'No way,' says Sid. 'But they do say a penicillin jab works wonders these days.'

I can't help feeling that Sid has misunderstood me but I decide not to labour the point.

The birds are all giggling away fit to bust and I see that they are taking a gander at the paintings on the wall. These are a bit fruity, to put it mildly. A lot of unencumbered knocker flying about and no sign of the spirit that makes the Festival of Light such a fine body of men and women. Our visitors obviously don't see a lot of this kind of thing in purdah – no telly, I suppose – and are revealing signs of being a very frisky load of fillies.

'I don't reckon they're getting enough,' says Sid.' Stands

to reason, doesn't it? I wonder how many of them each bloke has?'

'You can't judge by this lot,' I say. 'They're just here for the weekend, aren't they? I expect they've travelled light.'

Sid opens the door of the Hovell Room and stands to one side.

'Here we are, ladies-owch!'

I don't see what happens but Sid tells me later that he collected a more than friendly squeeze as the bints swept through the door.

'Gordon Bennett!' he says. 'I think I'd better go to the karsi and check stock. They don't take any prisoners, do they?'

When we get downstairs, a procession of Rolls-Royces has arrived outside the door and Sir Henry is doing the honours with a load of geezers in shawls and long woollen robes. They have curved daggers at their waists and look like the pictures on those boxes of dates that hang around so long at Christmas. You don't see a lot of them in the public bar of The Hand and Racket, I can tell you.

'. . . Abdul ben Krafti, Omar Gord.'

Omar Gord is really something if you go for the dark swarthy type and I notice that a startling change comes over Clarissa as she feasts her minces on him. She clasps her hands together and her mouth pops open as if trying to frame the letter O. She looks really knocked out.

'Greetings, Oh fair gazelle,' murmurs Omar dropping his lips on her mit. 'I find myself in Allah's favour when I can bask in the presence of such beauty.'

Sid nudges me. 'You've had that one, mate. He'll be blowing his hooter on her yashmak before the night is out, you mark my words.'

I don't like to concede that Sid might be right but there is no doubt that Omar Gord wields a powerful attraction. Clarissa blushes and places her hand over the kissed limb as if protecting it from dust. 'Thank you,' she murmurs.

Bloody wog bastard! I know it is very naughty, but I can't

help getting the needle when I see this geezer moving in on my bird. I have been sweating blood without so much as a 'how's your father?' and now Sheikh, Rattle and Roll gives her a bit of pantomime chat and she is lying on her back with her tongue hanging out. I can't see what she sees in him. Just because he is a prince, good looking, and worth a few million quid a week. What does that matter? Do women have no sense of values these days? It is all these old Vaselino films on the tele that are causing the trouble. You never had this kind of problem with Abbot and Costello.

'Lea, escort his excellency to his chamber.'

'He fancies a piss, does he?' I say. I know it is not going to go down well but when I take umbrage I don't mess about.

'Lea!'

'How dare you!!'

Omar's hand leaps to the handle of his dagger. 'This infidel dog must die!'

It occurs to me that I may have gone a bit far. Of course, it is not me that I am worried about, it is the future of the British Empire – or Brixton as it is sometimes called. I am only hiding under the hall table in case Omar is put off by the sight of blood.

'Out, Jackal! Cold steel awaits your vitals!'

I don't like the sound of that, do you? I know what I consider to be vital.

'Absolutely right!' says Clarissa who is bouncing up and down. 'Rip the ghastly little man to pieces. It will serve him jolly well right!'

That's nice, isn't it? I don't mind a bit of the cold shoulder but even a Lea can take a hint after a while. I don't think the bird really fancies me.

'Your Excellency, please. The man will be punished according to the rules of the country.' Thank goodness for the calm authoritative voice of the British foreign service – although, I would be feeling a little happier if Sir Henry was not crouched under the table beside me. At any second I am expecting to become Lea kebabs but fortunately winsome Wanda also springs to the rescue.

'Let me remove this unworthy creature from your sight,' she says grabbing me by the ear hole. 'Come, Lea. I have work for you.'

I keep closer to the lady than the seam in her knickers until we have rounded the bend in the stairs. At floor level Omar Gord's blazing eyes burn a hole in the back of my nut.

'Thanks, Wanda,' I say. 'I'll do the same for you, one day.'

'Be more careful in future,' she says. 'Otherwise, you won't have one.'

'Very well expressed,' I say. 'Well, I must—'

'Come here,' says Wanda. 'You haven't seen my bedroom have you?' It is not exactly the way Anna Neagle would have gone about things but in the circumstances I don't feel that I should grumble. After all, she did stop me being cut off in my primaries. But for her I might be trying to elbow my way into the front row of the Vienna Boys Choir.

'Facing south, is it?' I say.

By the time I get out of it I have faced south, west, east and north and every direction in between. Blimey, what a goer that Wanda Zonker is. If they are all like her back home the sea off Lithuania must be warm to the touch.

I have taken half a dozen unsteady paces away from Wanda's room when I remember that I have left my watch behind. I knock on the Rory but there is no answer. Can she have fallen asleep? Flattering but unlikely. That bird has more beans than a coffee plantation.

I open the door and stick my head round it. The room is empty! There are cameras all over the floor and the Trotskyst Song Book on the bed-side table – such all time greats as *The Sound of Mujik, Marx, he's Making Eyes at Me* and *Where the Boyars Are* – but no sign of Wanda. Where can she have gone? She could not have left the room by the door without me seeing her. Perhaps she has disappeared into the walls like Lady Baulkit. It is all very strange.

I think about it all afternoon while I help Renato in the

kitchen. Sir Henry has organised a big banquet for the Arab geezers and you would not cocoa the amount of nosh that is being prepared. Sucking pigs, quail, all that capon. It fair makes your mouth water.

While we slave in the kitchens, and Roughage slavers over cook in the pantry, the future of our glorious country is being decided round the conference table. I do hope everything works out all right because I like a happy ending, don't you?

'I'm afraid you're going to have to serve at the banquet,' says Sid. 'It's Arab style, no birds except entertainment, and don't cock it up.'

This is not news that cheers me. 'That bugger Gord is going to be there,' I say. 'He's got it in for me.'

'Really?' says Sid. 'How very considerate of him. I didn't know you needed help.'

'Stop messing about, Sid. I'm scared I tell you.'

'Don't be a nana. He probably won't recognise you. I expect we all look the same to him.'

I am not convinced but it is difficult to argue with Sid. Especially when he says that he will smash your face in if you don't do as you are told. I ask him why he can't be a waiter but he says that he is going to be busy 'behind the scenes'.

It is shortly before the banquet is due to begin that I am walking down the long corridor where the Arabs have their rooms. This is a bad place to be walking as I discover when a door opens and Omar Gord sticks his nut round it. Fortunately he hardly looks at me.

'Infidel dog', he booms. 'Bear this missif to the mistress Clarissa and tarry not upon the way lest I introduce your zabb to the gelding iron.'

I don't know what a zabb is but I reckon I can guess without rushing out to buy an Arab dictionary. 'Verily forsooth,' I murmur, burying my chin in my chest and extending a mit. If only the bloke wasn't cleaning his nails with that dagger.

I scurry off and have a good mind to take a shufti at the note. The only problem is that it is sealed with a dirty great blob of wax bearing an imprint like that which you see on the side of your local dust cart. It doesn't half pong as well – I mean, the note, not your local dust cart. Attar of roses, or something like that. I know that Mum has had a bottle for so long that it has changed colour.

When I hand the note to Clarissa, she rips it out of my hand so fast that it burns my fingers. I can't read what it says but from the look on her face, it is obviously good news.

'Did I ever tell you about my ancestor, Sir Richard Lea?' I say deciding that I had better get in fast. 'He was a very interesting man. He—'

'Oh, do go away, you disgusting little man!' snaps my erstwhile sweetheart. 'I find your presence utterly repellant.'

'Are you sure?' I ask. 'I mean, people do make mistakes.'

She slams the door in my face and at that moment I realise something very important. I never really liked her anyway. She was just leading me on and she got what was coming to her.

Half an hour later I bump into Lady Baulkit standing in the hall.

'Back to the dower house and an evening in front of the telly,' she says, looking round and running her fingers lightly up the inside of my leg. 'These staff affairs are a bore. I won't even have Clarissa for company. She's decided to be conscientious and stay here to ensure that everything is flowing smoothly.' She gazes deep into my eyes. 'What are you doing this evening?' Percy lunges forward eagerly like someone has shouted 'walkies!' but it is not to be.

'I'm waiting at the banquet,' I say, wearily.

'Another time.' She pats my cheek and drifts away. Gad, but life can be cruel sometimes, Carruthers.

The banquet is to be eaten Arab style and when I get into the huge room I see that there are blokes on top of poufs all over the place – don't get excited, Cedric! I am, of course, referring to the arrangements that have been made for parking your khyber. There is not a lot for me to do because most of the noshing is done with the mits. The guests get stuck in to whatever platters of goodies are dumped in front of them.

I am in charge of dishing out the booze and it comes as a surprise to me to see the Arabs knocking back the vino. I thought it was against their religion but this lot must be exempted. They are always sticking their horns in the air and asking for more.

Sir Henry looks a bit of a berk squatting uncomfortably on the floor in a dinner jacket but he seems happy enough.

'I think this day marks a giant step forward in Anglo-Arab relations,' he says to Abdul ben Krafti or one of his lot. The Arab burps in his face and slides a hand into his robe.

'You want to buy unspeakably feeeeeelthy photographs?' he says.

I leave them haggling happily and gaze around for more customers. Omar Gord is looking an absolute dream in a bejewelled cloak and a scimitar with precious stones as big as pigeons' eggs set in the handle. His cruel north and south twitches sardonically as his hooded minces dart round the birch broom. I think he has something else on his mind. I am trying to keep out of his way but he suddenly raises an arm and snaps his fingers. Clearly, he is seeking a drop of rise and shine.

Do you ever get the feeling that you know something is going to go wrong? Yes, so do I. I think Sir Henry does, too. There is a look almost of pleading in his eyes as I set off across the room. He fans himself with one of the photographs he has just bought – terrible they are. I don't know how they get camels to do things like that. I have heard of having the hump, but they are ridiculous.

'Here, dog!' They don't mind how they talk to you, these blokes. I would not object so much if they refrained from spitting date stones all over the carpet. Even Dad does not do things like that. And he certainly does not wipe his sticky fingers on the upholstery. Not when Mum is looking anyway.

'Faster, base ingrate!' I could really belt him one but my natural sense of patriotism and cowardice makes me hold myself in check. I hurry across the room and – OH! What a silly place to leave the tube of your hookah. I catch my foot in it and the jug of wine sails into Omar's lap. The bloke who was smoking the pipe gets his false gnashers jerked across the room but I am not worried about him.

'By Allah's beard! You will die for this, infidel dog!!' Omar springs to his feet and whips out his scimitar. There is a nasty stain on his lovely white robe and I can understand him being a bit narky, but surely this is over-reacting.

'Hang on a minute!' I say.

Swish!! The blade whistles past my ear hole. People are scrambling in all directions and I am one of them. Crunch!! A table turns in to firewood.

'I say, steady on,' says Sir Henry.

'Stop him!' I scream. 'He's trying to kill me.'

'Yes.' Sir Henry sounds thoughtful.

'Die, jackal!!'

My back is against the fireplace and I chuck myself to one side as Omar lunges at me. My heart is in my mouth and there is not much room for it because my stomach got there first. Thwack! The blade smites the wood work and immediately I hear a familiar grinding noise. I look behind me and see a panel sliding to one side. Omar must have activated the cherub's chopper.

I don't hang about but dart into the dark opening. Anywhere to get away from the mad mullah. It is as dark as a Nigerian's inside leg measurement but I press forward feeling the damp walls brushing my finger tips. Suddenly there is an opening to my left and I press into it. With any luck, Omar Gord will blunder past and I can escape. I can hear him effing and blinding behind me.

I hold my breath and his robes brush against me as he rushes on. The pong of perfume is so great as to make you think the bloke must have something to hide.

I am just beginning to treat myself to half a sigh of relief when – 'AAAAAAAAAAAAAARGH!!!' – SPLASH!!!!

Omar's voice disappears into something deep and wet – suggestions on a postcard, please. I can hear a muffled voice shouting in what I suppose is Arabic so he must be all right – well, sort of all right. I don't feel inclined to win a Humane Society award in the circumstances. Somebody else can get him out. Behind me are some steps and I start to feel my way up them.

In the distance is a pinpoint of light and the steps lead me to it. As I get closer, I realise that it might be one of the peep holes I took a shufti through with Lady Baulkit. I apply one of my minces and – blimey! There is a bloke lying on the bed surrounded by a load of naked birds wearing yashmaks.

'Careful, Fatima!' I hear him warn. 'You nearly bruised my lips with that grape.'

Sid! So that is why the crafty bugger said he was tied up. He is knocking off the harem girls while I act as wine waiter to a load of blood-crazed Arabs. What a mate he is. With a brother in law like him I don't need Omar practising opencast surgery. For two pins and the whereabouts of the secret panel, I would barge in and spoil his little gonads. I am about to bash on the wall and destroy his natural rhythm when the bird with the grapes suddenly flings them over her shoulder and buries her face in Sid's chest. Immediately, the rest of them leap on Clapham's answer to Paul Newman as if responding to a signal. I have never seen anything like it! He cries out, but his screams are drowned in a throbbing avalanche of female flesh. I would like to clock more but the curtains of the four poster come down and all I can see is what looks like a carpet beating contest. Goodness knows what is going on in there. I wait for a minute until the yelps become painful and then continue on my way. Even when it is Sid my natural sense of delicacy springs to the fore.

Another half-dozen faltering, fear-choked paces and I see rectangular line of light. It is as faint as Ted Heath's chances of dancing at Covent Garden but it does suggest the presence of some kind of door opening. I set my digits to work and at last feel a spring give beneath their touch. A panel slides back and a familiar niff invades my hooter. Attar of Omar. Can I have blundered into Gord's room?

No sooner has the unpleasant thought entered my nut than a familiar voice wafts into my lug-holes.

'Oh Omar. You've been using the back passage.'

The dicky birds issue from the shapely north and south of Clarissa Baulkit and I assume that they are upper class rabbit for taking a tom tit. What a funny thing to say to a bloke. I ponder about this but what really interests me is the thought that Omar has clearly invited Lady Baulkit's little girl round for a spot of hampton parking. I hear a bed spring squeak and realise that the saucy minx must have hopped into the Uncle Ned. You have to watch them these days, don't you?

'Omar?'

Of course, I must reveal myself, mustn't I? I can't have this nice girl in labour under a delusion. It would be so unkind, so ill bred, so repellant, so—

'Indeed, my little turtle dove,' I husk, making Paul Robeson sound like Petula Clark. 'The moment you have been waiting for has arrived.'

'Oh, Omar!'

I rip off my threads like they are on fire and make for Clarissa's voice. It is a pity about the chest in the middle of the room but I pick myself up and struggle on gamely.

'Are you all right?' I have never heard Clarissa sounding so concerned about anything.

'No force on earth can keep me from you. I speed to your side like the fastest desert cheetah.' Or cheater, maybe.

'Shall I turn on the light?'

'No,' I say hurriedly. 'It is not Allah's will.'

I pat the bed and – yes. There is Clarissa. Lucky girl. I run my germans down to her shapely rocks and boulders and feel her shiver. 'I've always dreamed of being made love to by an Arab chieftain,' she purrs.

'You will find it unbelievable,' I say, pulling back the sheets. 'Promise me one thing, though.'

'What is it?' she breathes.

'If the ecstasy becomes too unbearable, you must tell me.'

'Oh Omar!'

I slide between the sheets and sweep her into my Chalk Farms. I hope the real Omar is still having a swim otherwise it could become rather crowded in here. Clarissa is quivering like a piece of rafia tied to an electric fan and it obvious that a swift dose of my giggle stick is what she yearns. As I browse in the soft pastures of her neck her eager fingers col-side with percy and she sucks in her breath.

'It's huge,' she gasps.

'The ship of the desert,' I say. In fact, my action man kit is very much the standard model and Clarissa's reaction throws some interesting light on the powers of auto-sugges-tion. I let my hands race each other down her body, and gently check that her reception area is ready to receive its very important guest.

'Oh,' says Clarissa, very refined-like. 'Please try and insert it.'

'Verily,' I murmur. Rising to my knees, I position panting percy at the entrance to her grab-it hutch and slide my hands beneath her back bumpers. 'And now, as we say in the Casbah "Cop this."!'

I don't want to boast but I reckon that my distinguished ancestor, Sir Richard would have been proud of me. Even old Omar could have had few complaints. The bed is slomp-ing backwards and forwards like a leaking tub sinking in a gale.

'Now!' She gasps. 'Now, now, NOW!!!'

What an orgasm it is. The back of the bed falls off, she bites a lump out of my shoulder, three policemen break down the door and the light goes on. I don't recognise them as cops at first but the bloke with the dirty mac and the flash-light helps me.

'MacGoolygrab of the Yard,' he says, saluting me with his

flashlight and nearly knocking himself out. 'Sorry to barge in like this, Your Omnipotence, but we have reason to believe that a Russian spy is taking compromising photographs of you from the inside of this grandfather's clock.'

He wrenches open the door and we all watch the pendelum swinging from side to side. All except Clarissa. She looks at me and has hysterics.

'You don't mean Wanda Zonker, do you?' I ask, jumping to conclusions fast.

'*Comrade* Wanda Zonker,' corrects MacGoolygrab. 'Do you know her whereabouts?'

'I've had some experience of them,' I say guardedly. I mean, you have to be careful what you admit to the Fuzz these days. They are cracking down on everything.

'Have you any idea where she might be?' asks MacG.

'She might have escaped through one of the secret panels,' I say. 'Twist the balls of that little chap next to the fireplace.'

Immediately, MacGoolygrab assaults one of his men who collapses on the floor, screaming.

'Not him!' I screech. 'I meant the carved wooden cherub.' The three men, one of them hobbling, hurl themselves at the pannelling and after a few desperate seconds the secret passage is revealed.

'Mind you don't fall down the—' I call. But they have already gone.

Now I am alone with Clarissa again. She appears to have fainted. Her blonde hair falls across her shoulder and there is a beguiling blush tinting the perfect English rose complexion of her cheek. I examine the soft swellings of her breasts and the dainty curve of her alabaster belly. Only an animal would take advantage of her in this condition.

'Woof, woof!' I say, scrambling to my knees.

## CHAPTER 10

**In which we learn some startling information about Wanda Zonker and Timmy and Sid are forced to move on.**

'"Once again, Western Civilization trembles on edge of abyss." That's nice, isn't it?' says Sid, putting down the paper.

'How did she get in to it?' I ask.

'"Abyss", Timmo, "abyss". The bottomless bowels not the lady abbots.'

'How can you have bowels without a bottom, Sid?'

Sid sighs and pushes away his cornflakes. 'I'm not in the mood for dialectic, today,' he says. 'Gordon Bennett! Who's been using the malt extract spoon in the sugar bowl?'

'That's Marmite,' I say. 'I was finishing up the jar.'

Sid sniffs the spoon and then tastes it. 'Yeah, you're right. Diabolical.'

'What I don't understand is why they printed all those photographs,' I say.

'For precisely the reason that is stated in this headline,' says Sid. 'It undermines confidence in our way of life, doesn't it? When you see cabinet ministers behaving in the same way as the rest of the people it makes you bubble with righteous disgust. It also helped put the kibosh on the oil deal, didn't it – that and you.'

'It's amazing how they all ended up in the Baltic, isn't it?'

'Those North Sea currents are very funny, Timmo. I've read about them.'

'I was very surprised to learn about the subterranean river leading out in to the channel.'

'Yes, thank goodness Inspector MacGoolygrab and his men were able to use their truncheons as the basis of a flimsy raft.'

'It's amazing what they teach them at Hendon, these days.'

'Amazing.'

There is a pause in which I try not to listen to Sid drinking his tea.

'And so fortunate to catch up with Omar Gord. I hear that the weight of his burnous was beginning to pull him down.'

'I believe they do have big ones.'

'He was furious about being picked up by Moshe Dayan's private yacht.'

'They're a very sensitive race, Timmo. But then, I don't have to tell you that.'

I nod my head. 'I wonder where Wanda is now?'

'Behind the iron curtain, I expect. Or working for Playboy. Probably both.'

'I never got paid for any of those photographs, you know.'

'It would be against her Communist principles, wouldn't it?'

A faraway look comes into Sid's eyes. 'I had a little flutter with her, you know.'

I think about the canopy falling off the four poster. 'These things happen, Sid. Ships that pass in the night.'

'What's that got to do with it?'

'I said "ships", Sid.'

'Oh yeah. I thought you meant—'

'It's Sir Henry I feel sorry for,' I say hurriedly.

'I feel sorry for us all,' says Sid. 'I mean, after the "British Government Runs Health Farm Brothel For Arab Envoys" scandal had broken we all thought we were going to be out of business, didn't we? We didn't know that people would be trampled to death in the rush to get into the place.'

'And then for it to be burnt down.'

'A tragedy,' says Sid. 'And what a way for it to happen. The sparks from the studs on that copper's boot igniting the toilet roll when he was standing on the holder looking in the cistern, I could have understood it if it had happened when they were using the blow lamp to see if there were any clues hidden in the frame of the Rembrandt.'

'Still, I expect Sir Henry's lecture tour of America will be a big success.'

'If he can get a visor, Timmo.'

'Don't you mean a visa, Sid?'

'With his mug, he needs a visor before he'll be able to get a visa.' Sid knocks back his tea and wipes his mouth with the back of his hand. 'Clarissa dropped the rape charges, has she?'

'Yeah. Her lawyer reckoned it wouldn't stand up in court.'

'You'd have been in dead stuck if it had done, wouldn't you? They'd have put you away immediately.' Sid stands up and blows on his mits. 'Come on. We'd better go and look for firewood. Thanks to you we've got another bleeding ten wears of this freezing misery.' He walks to the door rubbing his hands together. 'We might drop in at The Highwayman on the way back. There's an idea I want to talk to you about . . .'

# ONWARD VIRGINS

## Oliver Grape

# LOSE MY VIRGINITY? - I COULDN'T GIVE IT AWAY WITH BLUESHIELD STAMPS!

It is not surprising with some of the handicaps I have. A Dad who builds a cabin cruiser called 'Spirit of Wormwood Scrubs' in the back garden – and can't get it out. A competition-mad Mum who is always filling the house with crates of baked beans – and that's just to go in for the competitions. A sister who can run faster than any boy in the neighbourhood – there isn't one who's got away from her yet. A brother who makes David Bowie look like a square, and Gran – Hitler in skirts.

It is no wonder that I'm a bit uneasy in my relationship with girls: Angie who doesn't want to know, Sandra who knows too much, hot-blooded Caroline, Cherilyn who is on the cards, Mrs Lewis who is on the game, available Greer and Pat who is passing through. It's a blooming miracle that the story has a happy ending.

# CONFESSIONS FROM THE POP SCENE

## Timothy Lea

Teenyboppers, hungry groupies, payola, crooked DJs, foreign tours, golden discs, TV spectaculars, screaming fans and packed out concert halls...

For Timmy Lea, always on the lookout for a new career with plenty of openings, Noggo Enterprises spelled success, money and a chance to get his name into the bright lights – providing he could survive the partnership with brother-in-law Sid and his nephew Jason Noggett, the 7-year-old's answer to Mick Jagger, not to speak of Dyke Henna, the transvestite rock star (born Fred Nudger).

Even when business was slow, the manager of Noggo Enterprises found plenty of scope for his talents; in beds, bars and the back seats of sportscars there was always somebody who wanted a little piece of his action.

Would simple, unaffected Timmy survive in the hard world of Pop?

## *CONFESSIONS OF A NIGHT NURSE*

### *Rosie Dixon*

**IT WASN'T SO MUCH A QUESTION OF LOSING HER VIRGINITY AS OF MISLAYING IT.**

**Rosie Dixon really did want to save herself for Mr. Right but things had a habit of getting on top of her. Like that party which got out of hand and made her parents so angry they asked her to leave home.**

**Not to worry. Queen Adelaide's Hospital always had room for a warmhearted girl with a willing pair of hands.**

**At a big hospital like that she couldn't help bumping into men. Rosie soon made a name for herself as every patient's dream, matron's nightmare and doctor's dilemma.**

# The Reluctant Musketeer

## Anthony Burton

A Story of National Service

2763418 Aircraftman Second Class Grant had no ambitions to come top of the class, win promotion or, God forbid, win any medals. He just wanted to survive his National Service stint as painlessly as he could.

The accommodating Rita, nicknamed the camp bicycle ("because everyone rode her"), certainly helped to ease the pain; as did Mavis and Cynthia, the baton twirling, hip swaying drum majorettes of the Calgary High School Band.

Unfortunately Grant also had a talent for getting himself into trouble. His two years with the RAF turned into a riot of misadventures with the randy Irishman Paddy Ferguson, the incurable air-sick Ellie and the lunatic Eric Wade who took to dressing in women's clothes to prove he wasn't queer. It took them from the frozen prairies of Canada to the blistering heat of Cyprus . . . and finally to the ludicrous climax of the Suez War, codename Operation Musketeer.

CHARLES DENNIS

# STONED COLD SOLDIER
## CHARLES DENNIS

The most savage and scurrilous satire on war since CATCH 22 and M*A*S*H.
'Beautifully managed. A very funny book made funnier by a passionate indignation'.
THE TIMES

When the men of 'B' Company's Wichita platoon simply vanished into thin air, a lot of people started asking awkward questions. David Maxwell, ace reporter and darling of the T.V. networks, a man terrified that it was his destiny to get crabs and die, was sent to find the answers.

What was the purpose of the outsize quonset hut that appeared overnight at the edge of the jungle? Why did the army deny that the camp's medic, Dr. Markson, ever existed? Why did Father Doolan carry a revolver? What was the role of Cashbox, the exquisite $100 whore? Why was 'the Murder Man' sent out to Saigon? Who was Chy Ming?

It began as a mystery: it ended as a scandal that could rock the Pentagon.

**'Carries all along in a torrent of scurrilous abuse. He loves words and uses them like bullets from a machine-gun.'**
**THE SPECTATOR**

**'Ingenious . . . a really good tale'.**
**SUNDAY TIMES**

# VIZZINI

## THE SECRET LIFE OF AMERICA'S NO. 1 UNDERCOVER AGENT BY SAL VIZZINI

**In the course of his extraordinary career Sal Vizzini was shot three times, knifed twice, savagely beaten up and has had several contracts put out by the Mafia to kill him.**

**His story packs into one book enough material for a whole series of novels. As an undercover agent for the F.B.I., he was assigned to Naples where he became a 'friend' of exiled Mafia chieftain Charles 'Lucky' Luciano; to Burma, where he blew up a heroin factory; to Lebanon, where he outwitted a Communist gun-running ring; and to Atlanta, Georgia, where he posed as a con in the Federal Pen in order to find out where a million dollars in government bonds had been hidden by a prisoner.**